D1061320

THE GOODNESS OF ST. ROCQUE
AND OTHER STORIES

The GOODNESS OF ST. ROCQUE
AND OTHER STORIES

By

A L I C E   D U N B A R

New York: DODD, MEAD AND COMPANY   *Mdcccxcix*

McGrath Publishing Company
College Park, Maryland

Reprint McGrath Publishing Company 1969
Reprinted from the copy in the Harvard College Library

Library of Congress Catalog Card Number: 76-76103

Manufactured in the United States of America
by Arno Press, Inc., New York

To
My best Comrade
My Husband

CONTENTS

THE GOODNESS OF SAINT ROCQUE

1

THE GOODNESS OF SAINT ROCQUE

MANUELA was tall and slender and graceful, and once you knew her the lithe form could never be mistaken. She walked with the easy spring that comes from a perfectly arched foot. To-day she swept swiftly down Marais Street, casting a quick glance here and there from under her heavy veil as if she feared she was being followed. If you had peered under the veil, you would have seen that Manuela's dark eyes were swollen and discoloured about the lids, as though they had known a sleepless, tearful night.

There had been a picnic the day before, and as merry a crowd of giddy, chattering Creole girls and boys as

ever you could see boarded the ram-
shackle dummy-train that puffed its
way wheezily out wide Elysian Fields
Street, around the lily-covered bayous,
to Milneburg-on-the-Lake.   Now, a
picnic at Milneburg is a thing to be
remembered for ever.   One charters a
rickety-looking, weather-beaten danc-
ing-pavilion, built over the water, and
after storing the children — for your
true Creole never leaves the small folks
at home — and the baskets and mothers
downstairs, the young folks go up-
stairs and dance to the tune of the best
band you ever heard.   For what can
equal the music of a violin, a guitar, a
cornet, and a bass viol to trip the quadrille to at a picnic ?

Then one can fish in the lake and go
bathing under the prim bath-houses,
so severely separated sexually, and go
rowing on the lake in a trim boat, followed by the shrill warnings of anx-

ious mamans.   And in the evening one comes home, hat crowned with cool gray Spanish moss, hands burdened with fantastic latanier baskets woven by the brown bayou boys, hand in hand with your dearest one, tired but happy.

At this particular picnic, however, there had been bitterness of spirit. Theophilé was Manuela's own especial property, and Theophilé had proven false. He had not danced a single waltz or quadrille with Manuela, but had deserted her for Claralie, blonde and petite. It was Claralie whom Theophilé had rowed out on the lake; it was Claralie whom Theophilé had gallantly led to dinner; it was Claralie's hat that he wreathed with Spanish moss, and Claralie whom he escorted home after the jolly singing ride in town on the little dummy-train.

Not that Manuela lacked partners or admirers.   Dear no ! she was too graceful and beautiful for that. There had been more than enough for her. But Manuela loved Theophilé, you see, and no one could take his place. Still, she had tossed her head and let her silvery laughter ring out in the dance, as though she were the happiest of mortals, and had tripped home with Henri, leaning on his arm, and looking up into his eyes as though she adored him.

This morning she showed the traces of a sleepless night and an aching heart as she walked down Marais Street. Across wide St. Rocque Avenue she hastened. " Two blocks to the river and one below —" she repeated to herself breathlessly. Then she stood on the corner gazing about her, until with a final summoning of a desperate courage she dived through a small wicket gate into a garden of weed-choked flowers.

There was a hoarse, rusty little bell on the gate that gave querulous tongue as she pushed it open. The house that sat back in the yard was little and old and weather-beaten. Its one-story frame had once been painted, but that was a memory remote and traditional. A straggling morning-glory strove to conceal its time-ravaged face. The little walk of broken bits of brick was reddened carefully, and the one little step was scrupulously yellow-washed, which denoted that the occupants were cleanly as well as religious.

Manuela's timid knock was answered by a harsh " Entrez."

It was a small sombre room within, with a bare yellow-washed floor and ragged curtains at the little window. In a corner was a diminutive altar draped with threadbare lace. The red glow of the taper lighted a cheap print of St. Joseph and a brazen crucifix. The

human element in the room was fur-
nished by a little, wizened yellow
woman, who, black-robed, turbaned,
and stern, sat before an uncertain table
whereon were greasy cards.

Manuela paused, her eyes blinking
at the semi-obscurity within.   The
Wizened One called in croaking tones :
"An' fo' w'y you come here ? Assiez-
là, ma'amzelle."

Timidly Manuela sat at the table
facing the owner of the voice.

" I want," she began faintly ; but the
Mistress of the Cards understood : she
had had much experience.   The cards
were shuffled in her long grimy talons
and stacked before Manuela.

" Now you cut dem in t'ree part,
so — un, deux, trois, bien ! You mek'
you' weesh wid all you' heart, bien !
Yaas, I see, I see !"

Breathlessly did Manuela learn that
her lover was true, but " dat light gal,

yaas, she mek' nouvena in St. Rocque fo' hees love."

"I give you one lil' charm, yaas," said the Wizened One when the séance was over, and Manuela, all white and nervous, leaned back in the rickety chair. "I give you one lil' charm fo' to ween him back, yaas. You wear h'it 'roun' you' wais', an' he come back. Den you mek prayer at St. Rocque an' burn can'le. Den you come back an' tell me, yaas. Cinquante sous, ma'amzelle. Merci. Good luck go wid you."

Readjusting her veil, Manuela passed out the little wicket gate, treading on air. Again the sun shone, and the breath of the swamps came as healthful sea-breeze unto her nostrils. She fairly flew in the direction of St. Rocque.

There were quite a number of persons entering the white gates of

the cemetery, for this was Friday,
when all those who wish good luck
pray to the saint, and wash their steps
promptly at twelve o'clock with a
wondrous mixture to guard the house.
Manuela bought a candle from the
keeper of the little lodge at the entrance, and pausing one instant by the
great sun-dial to see if the heavens and
the hour were propitious, glided into
the tiny chapel, dim and stifling with
heavy air from myriad wish-candles
blazing on the wide table before the
altar-rail.   She said her prayer and
lighting her candle placed it with the
others.

Mon Dieu! how brightly the sun
seemed to shine now, she thought,
pausing at the door on her way out.
Her small finger-tips, still bedewed with
holy water, rested caressingly on a
gamin's head.   The ivy which enfolds
the quaint chapel never seemed so

green; the shrines which serve as the Way of the Cross never seemed so artistic; the baby graves, even, seemed cheerful.

Theophilé called Sunday. Manuela's heart leaped. He had been spending his Sundays with Claralie. His stay was short and he was plainly bored. But Manuela knelt to thank the good St. Rocque that night, and fondled the charm about her slim waist. There came a box of bonbons during the week, with a decorative card all roses and fringe, from Theophilé; but being a Creole, and therefore superstitiously careful, and having been reared by a wise and experienced maman to mistrust the gifts of a recreant lover, Manuela quietly thrust bonbons, box, and card into the kitchen fire, and the Friday following placed the second candle of her nouvena in St. Rocque.

Those of Manuela's friends who had

watched with indignation Théophilé
gallantly leading Claralie home from
High Mass on Sundays, gasped with
astonishment when the next Sunday,
with his usual bow, the young man
offered Manuela his arm as the wor-
shippers filed out in step to the
organ's march. Claralie tossed her
head as she crossed herself with holy
water, and the pink in her cheeks was
brighter than usual.

Manuela smiled a bright good-morn-
ing when she met Claralie in St. Rocque
the next Friday. The little blonde
blushed furiously, and Manuela rushed
post-haste to the Wizened One to
confer upon this new issue.

"H'it ees good," said the dame, shaking her turbaned head. "She ees 'fraid,
she will work, mais you' charm, h'it
weel beat her."

And Manuela departed with radiant
eyes.

Theophilé was not at Mass Sunday morning, and murderous glances flashed from Claralie to Manuela before the tinkling of the Host-Bell. Nor did Theophilé call at either house. Two hearts beat furiously at the sound of every passing footstep, and two minds wondered if the other were enjoying the beloved one's smiles. Two pair of eyes, however, blue and black, smiled on others, and their owners laughed and seemed none the less happy. For your Creole girls are proud, and would die rather than let the world see their sorrows.

Monday evening Theophilé, the missing, showed his rather sheepish countenance in Manuela's parlour, and explained that he, with some chosen spirits, had gone for a trip — " over the Lake."

" I did not ask you where you were yesterday," replied the girl, saucily.

Theophilé shrugged his shoulders and changed the conversation.

The next week there was a birthday fête in honour of Louise, Theophilé's young sister. Everyone was bidden, and no one thought of refusing, for Louise was young, and this would be her first party. So, though the night was hot, the dancing went on as merrily as light young feet could make it go. Claralie fluffed her dainty white skirts, and cast mischievous sparkles in the direction of Theophilé, who with the maman and Louise was bravely trying not to look self-conscious. Manuela, tall and calm and proud-looking, in a cool, pale yellow gown was apparently enjoying herself without paying the slightest attention to her young host.

" Have I the pleasure of this dance ? " he asked her finally, in a lull of the music.

She bowed assent, and as if moved

by a common impulse they strolled out of the dancing-room into the cool, quaint garden, where jessamines gave out an overpowering perfume, and a caged mocking-bird complained melodiously to the full moon in the sky.

It must have been an engrossing tête-a-tête, for the call to supper had sounded twice before they heard and hurried into the house. The march had formed with Louise radiantly leading on the arm of papa. Claralie tripped by with Leon. Of course, nothing remained for Theophilé and Manuela to do but to bring up the rear, for which they received much good-natured chaffing.

But when the party reached the dining-room, Theophilé proudly led his partner to the head of the table, at the right hand of maman, and smiled benignly about at the delighted assemblage. Now you know, when a Creole young man places a girl at his mother's right hand at his own table, there is but one conclusion to be deduced therefrom.

If you had asked Manuela, after the wedding was over, how it happened, she would have said nothing, but looked wise.

If you had asked Claralie, she would have laughed and said she always preferred Leon.

If you had asked Theophilé, he would have wondered that you thought he had ever meant more than to tease Manuela.

If you had asked the Wizened One, she would have offered you a charm.

But St. Rocque knows, for he is a good saint, and if you believe in him and are true and good, and make your nouvenas with a clean heart, he will grant your wish.

TONY'S WIFE

TONY'S WIFE

"GIMME fi' cents worth o' candy, please." It was the little Jew girl who spoke, and Tony's wife roused herself from her knitting to rise and count out the multi-hued candy which should go in exchange for the dingy nickel grasped in warm, damp fingers. Three long sticks, carefully wrapped in crispest brown paper, and a half dozen or more of pink candy fish for lagniappe, and the little Jew girl sped away in blissful contentment. Tony's wife resumed her knitting with a stifled sigh until the next customer should come.

A low growl caused her to look up apprehensively. Tony himself stood beetle-browed and huge in the small doorway.

" Get up from there," he muttered, " and open two dozen oysters right away; the Eliots want 'em." His English was unaccented. It was long since he had seen Italy.

She moved meekly behind the counter, and began work on the thick shells. Tony stretched his long neck up the street.

" Mr. Tony, mama wants some charcoal." The very small voice at his feet must have pleased him, for his black brows relaxed into a smile, and he poked the little one's chin with a hard, dirty finger, as he emptied the ridiculously small bucket of charcoal into the child's bucket, and gave a banana for lagniappe.

The crackling of shells went on behind, and a stifled sob arose as a bit of sharp edge cut into the thin, worn fingers that clasped the knife.

" Hurry up there, will you ? "

growled the black brows; "the Eliots
are sending for the oysters."

She deftly strained and counted
them, and, after wiping her fingers,
resumed her seat, and took up the endless crochet work, with her usual stifled
sigh.

Tony and his wife had always been
in this same little queer old shop on
Prytania Street, at least to the memory
of the oldest inhabitant in the neighbourhood. When or how they came, or
how they stayed, no one knew ; it was
enough that they were there, like a sort
of ancestral fixture to the street. The
neighbourhood was fine enough to look
down upon these two tumble-down
shops at the corner, kept by Tony
and Mrs. Murphy, the grocer. It was
a semi-fashionable locality, far up-town,
away from the old-time French quarter.
It was the sort of neighbourhood where
millionaires live before their fortunes are

made and fashionable, high-priced private schools flourish, where the small cottages are occupied by aspiring school-teachers and choir-singers. Such was this locality, and you must admit that it was indeed a condescension to tolerate Tony and Mrs. Murphy.

He was a great, black-bearded, hoarse-voiced, six-foot specimen of Italian humanity, who looked in his little shop and on the prosaic pavement of Prytania Street somewhat as Hercules might seem in a modern drawing-room. You instinctively thought of wild mountain-passes, and the gleaming dirks of bandit contadini in looking at him. What his last name was, no one knew. Someone had maintained once that he had been christened Antonio Malatesta, but that was unauthentic, and as little to be believed as that other wild theory that her name was Mary.

She was meek, pale, little, ugly, and German. Altogether part of his arms and legs would have very decently made another larger than she. Her hair was pale and drawn in sleek, thin tightness away from a pinched, pitiful face, whose dull cold eyes hurt you, because you knew they were trying to mirror sorrow, and could not because of their expressionless quality. No matter what the weather or what her other toilet, she always wore a thin little shawl of dingy brick-dust hue about her shoulders. No matter what the occasion or what the day, she always carried her knitting with her, and seldom ceased the incessant twist, twist of the shining steel among the white cotton meshes. She might put down the needles and lace into the spool-box long enough to open oysters, or wrap up fruit and candy, or count out wood and coal into infinitesimal portions, or do her housework; but the knitting was snatched with avidity at the first spare moment, and the worn, white, blue-marked fingers, half enclosed in kid-glove stalls for protection, would writhe and twist in and out again. Little girls just learning to crochet borrowed their patterns from Tony's wife, and it was considered quite a mark of advancement to have her inspect a bit of lace done by eager, chubby fingers. The ladies in larger houses, whose husbands would be millionaires some day, bought her lace, and gave it to their servants for Christmas presents.

As for Tony, when she was slow in opening his oysters or in cooking his red beans and spaghetti, he roared at her, and prefixed picturesque adjectives to her lace, which made her hide it under her apron with a fearsome look in her dull eyes.

He hated her in a lusty, roaring fashion, as a healthy beefy boy hates a sick cat and torments it to madness. When she displeased him, he beat her, and knocked her frail form on the floor. The children could tell when this had happened. Her eyes would be red, and there would be blue marks on her face and neck. "Poor Mrs. Tony," they would say, and nestle close to her. Tony did not roar at her for petting them, perhaps, because they spent money on the multi-hued candy in glass jars on the shelves.

Her mother appeared upon the scene once, and stayed a short time; but Tony got drunk one day and beat her because she ate too much, and she disappeared soon after. Whence she came and where she departed, no one could tell, not even Mrs. Murphy, the Pauline Pry and Gazette of the block.

Tony had gout, and suffered for

many days in roaring helplessness, the while his foot, bound and swathed in many folds of red flannel, lay on the chair before him. In proportion as his gout increased and he bawled from pure physical discomfort, she became light-hearted, and moved about the shop with real, brisk cheeriness. He could not hit her then without such pain that after one or two trials he gave up in disgust.

So the dull years had passed, and life had gone on pretty much the same for Tony and the German wife and the shop. The children came on Sunday evenings to buy the stick candy, and on week-days for coal and wood. The servants came to buy oysters for the larger houses, and to gossip over the counter about their employers. The little dry woman knitted, and the big man moved lazily in and out in his red flannel shirt, exchanged politics with

the tailor next door through the window, or lounged into Mrs. Murphy's
bar and drank fiercely. Some of the
children grew up and moved away, and
other little girls came to buy candy and
eat pink lagniappe fishes, and the shop
still thrived.

One day Tony was ill, more than the
mummied foot of gout, or the wheeze
of asthma ; he must keep his bed and
send for the doctor.

She clutched his arm when he came,
and pulled him into the tiny room.

" Is it — is it anything much, doctor ? " she gasped.

Æsculapius shook his head as wisely
as the occasion would permit. She
followed him out of the room into the
shop.

" Do you — will he get well, doctor ? "

Æsculapius buttoned up his frock
coat, smoothed his shining hat, cleared
his throat, then replied oracularly,

" Madam, he is completely burned out inside. Empty as a shell, madam, empty as a shell. He cannot live, for he has nothing to live on."

As the cobblestones rattled under the doctor's equipage rolling leisurely up Prytania Street, Tony's wife sat in her chair and laughed, — laughed with a hearty joyousness that lifted the film from the dull eyes and disclosed a sparkle beneath.

The drear days went by, and Tony lay like a veritable Samson shorn of his strength, for his voice was sunken to a hoarse, sibilant whisper, and his black eyes gazed fiercely from the shock of hair and beard about a white face. Life went on pretty much as before in the shop; the children paused to ask how Mr. Tony was, and even hushed the jingles on their bell hoops as they passed the door. Red-headed Jimmie, Mrs. Murphy's nephew, did the hard jobs, such as splitting wood and lifting coal from the bin; and in the intervals between tending the fallen giant and waiting on the customers, Tony's wife sat in her accustomed chair, knitting fiercely, with an inscrutable smile about her purple compressed mouth.

Then John came, introducing himself, serpent-wise, into the Eden of her bosom.

John was Tony's brother, huge and bluff too, but fair and blond, with the beauty of Northern Italy. With the same lack of race pride which Tony had displayed in selecting his German spouse, John had taken unto himself Betty, a daughter of Erin, aggressive, powerful, and cross-eyed. He turned up now, having heard of this illness, and assumed an air of remarkable authority at once.

A hunted look stole into the dull eyes, and after John had departed with blustering directions as to Tony's welfare, she crept to his bedside timidly.

"Tony," she said,—"Tony, you are very sick."

An inarticulate growl was the only response.

"Tony, you ought to see the priest; you must n't go any longer without taking the sacrament."

The growl deepened into words.

"Don't want any priest; you 're always after some snivelling old woman's fuss. You and Mrs. Murphy go on with your church; it won't make *you* any better."

She shivered under this parting shot, and crept back into the shop. Still the priest came next day.

She followed him in to the bedside and knelt timidly.

"Tony," she whispered, "here 's Father Leblanc."

Tony was too languid to curse out

loud; he only expressed his hate in a toss of the black beard and shaggy mane.

"Tony," she said nervously, "won't you do it now? It won't take long, and it will be better for you when you go— Oh, Tony, don't—don't laugh. Please, Tony, here's the priest."

But the Titan roared aloud: "No; get out. Think I'm a-going to give you a chance to grab my money now? Let me die and go to hell in peace."

Father Leblanc knelt meekly and prayed, and the woman's weak pleadings continued, —

"Tony, I've been true and good and faithful to you. Don't die and leave me no better than before. Tony, I do want to be a good woman once, a real-for-true married woman. Tony, here's the priest; say yes." And she wrung her ringless hands.

"You want my money," said Tony,

slowly, "and you sha'n't have it, not a cent; John shall have it."

Father Leblanc shrank away like a fading spectre. He came next day and next day, only to see re-enacted the same piteous scene,—the woman pleading to be made a wife ere death hushed Tony's blasphemies, the man chuckling in pain-racked glee at the prospect of her bereaved misery. Not all the prayers of Father Leblanc nor the wailings of Mrs. Murphy could alter the determination of the will beneath the shock of hair; he gloated in his physical weakness at the tenacious grasp on his mentality.

"Tony," she wailed on the last day, her voice rising to a shriek in its eagerness, "tell them I'm your wife; it'll be the same. Only say it, Tony, before you die!"

He raised his head, and turned stiff eyes and gibbering mouth on her; then,

with one chill finger pointing at John,
fell back dully and heavily.

They buried him with many honours
by the Society of Italia's Sons.   John
took possession of the shop when they
returned home, and found the money
hidden in the chimney corner.

As for Tony's wife, since she was not
his wife after all, they sent her forth in
the world penniless, her worn fingers
clutching her bundle of clothes in nervous agitation, as though they regretted
the time lost from knitting.

THE FISHERMAN OF PASS CHRISTIAN

THE FISHERMAN OF PASS CHRISTIAN.

THE swift breezes on the beach at Pass Christian meet and conflict as though each strove for the mastery of the air. The land-breeze blows down through the pines, resinous, fragrant, cold, bringing breath-like memories of dim, dark woods shaded by myriad pine-needles. The breeze from the Gulf is warm and soft and languorous, blowing up from the south with its suggestion of tropical warmth and passion. It is strong and masterful, and tossed Annette's hair and whipped her skirts about her in bold disregard for the proprieties.

Arm in arm with Philip, she was strolling slowly down the great pier which extends from the Mexican Gulf

Hotel into the waters of the Sound. There was no moon to-night, but the sky glittered and scintillated with myriad stars, brighter than you can ever see farther North, and the great waves that the Gulf breeze tossed up in restless profusion gleamed with the white fire of phosphorescent flame. The wet sands on the beach glowed white fire; the posts of the pier where the waves had leapt and left a laughing kiss, the sides of the little boats and fish-cars tugging at their ropes, alike showed white and flaming, as though the sea and all it touched were afire.

Annette and Philip paused midway the pier to watch two fishermen casting their nets. With heads bared to the breeze, they stood in clear silhouette against the white background of sea.

"See how he uses his teeth," almost whispered Annette.

Drawing himself up to his full height,

with one end of the huge seine between his teeth, and the cord in his left hand, the taller fisherman of the two paused a half instant, his right arm extended, grasping the folds of the net. There was a swishing rush through the air, and it settled with a sort of sob as it cut the waters and struck a million sparkles of fire from the waves. Then, with backs bending under the strain, the two men swung on the cord, drawing in the net, laden with glittering restless fish, which were unceremoniously dumped on the boards to be put into the fish-car awaiting them.

Philip laughingly picked up a soft, gleaming jelly-fish, and threatened to put it on Annette's neck. She screamed, ran, slipped on the wet boards, and in another instant would have fallen over into the water below. The tall fisherman caught her in his arms and set her on her feet.

"Mademoiselle must be very careful," he said in the softest and most correct French. "The tide is in and the water very rough. It would be very difficult to swim out there to-night."

Annette murmured confused thanks, which were supplemented by Philip's hearty tones. She was silent until they reached the pavilion at the end of the pier. The semi-darkness was unrelieved by lantern or light. The strong wind wafted the strains from a couple of mandolins, a guitar, and a tenor voice stationed in one corner to sundry engrossed couples in sundry other corners. Philip found an untenanted nook and they ensconced themselves therein.

"Do you know there's something mysterious about that fisherman?" said Annette, during a lull in the wind.

"Because he did not let you go over?" inquired Philip.

"No; he spoke correctly, and with the accent that goes only with an excellent education."

Philip shrugged his shoulders. "That's nothing remarkable. If you stay about Pass Christian for any length of time, you'll find more things than perfect French and courtly grace among fishermen to surprise you. These are a wonderful people who live across the Lake."

Annette was lolling in the hammock under the big catalpa-tree some days later, when the gate opened, and Natalie's big sun-bonnet appeared. Natalie herself was discovered blushing in its dainty depths. She was only a little Creole seaside girl, you must know, and very shy of the city demoiselles. Natalie's patois was quite as different from Annette's French as it was from the postmaster's English.

"Mees Annette," she began, peony-

hued all over at her own boldness,
" we will have one lil' hay-ride this
night, and a fish-fry at the end.   Will
you come? "

Annette sprang to her feet in delight.
" Will I come? Certainly. How delightful! You are so good to ask me.
What shall—what time—" But Natalie's pink bonnet had fled precipitately
down the shaded walk.   Annette
laughed joyously as Philip lounged
down the gallery.

" I frightened the child away," she
told him.

You've never been for a hay-ride
and fish-fry on the shores of the Mississippi Sound, have you? When the
summer boarders and the Northern
visitors undertake to give one, it is a
comparatively staid affair, where due
regard is had for one's wearing apparel,
and where there are servants to do the
hardest work.   Then it is n't enjoyable

at all. But when the natives, the boys and girls who live there, make up their minds to have fun, you may depend upon its being just the best kind.

This time there were twenty boys and girls, a mamma or so, several papas, and a grizzled fisherman to restrain the ardor of the amateurs. The cart was vast and solid, and two comfortable, sleepy-looking mules constituted the drawing power. There were also tin horns, some guitars, an accordeon, and a quartet of much praised voices. The hay in the bottom of the wagon was freely mixed with pine needles, whose prickiness through your hose was amply compensated for by its delicious fragrance.

After a triumphantly noisy passage down the beach one comes to the stretch of heavy sand that lies between Pass Christian proper and Henderson's

Point. This is a hard pull for the
mules, and the more ambitious riders
get out and walk.   Then, after a final
strain through the shifting sands, bravo!
the shell road is reached, and one goes
cheering through the pine-trees to
Henderson's Point.

If ever you go to Pass Christian, you
must have a fish-fry at Henderson's
Point.   It is the pine-thicketed, white-
beached peninsula jutting out from the
land, with one side caressed by the
waters of the Sound and the other
purred over by the blue waves of the
Bay of St. Louis.   Here is the beginning of the great three-mile trestle
bridge to the town of Bay St. Louis,
and to-night from the beach could be
seen the lights of the villas glittering
across the Bay like myriads of unsleep-
ing eyes.

Here upon a firm stretch of white
sand camped the merry-makers.   Soon

a great fire of driftwood and pine
cones tossed its flames defiantly at a
radiant moon in the sky, and the fishers
were casting their nets in the sea.   The
more daring of the girls waded bare-
legged in the water, holding pine-
torches, spearing flounders and peering
for soft-shell crabs.

Annette had wandered farther in the
shallow water than the rest.   Suddenly
she stumbled against a stone, the torch
dropped and spluttered at her feet.
With a little helpless cry she looked
at the stretch of unfamiliar beach and
water to find herself all alone.

"Pardon me, mademoiselle," said a
voice at her elbow; "you are in dis-
tress?"

It was her fisherman, and with a
scarce conscious sigh of relief, Annette
put her hand into the outstretched
one at her side.

"I was looking for soft shells," she

explained, "and lost the crowd, and now my torch is out."

"Where is the crowd?" There was some amusement in the tone, and Annette glanced up quickly, prepared to be thoroughly indignant at this fisherman who dared make fun at her; but there was such a kindly look about his mouth that she was reassured and said meekly,—

"At Henderson's Point."

"You have wandered a half-mile away," he mused, "and have nothing to show for your pains but very wet skirts. If mademoiselle will permit me, I will take her to her friends, but allow me to suggest that mademoiselle will leave the water and walk on the sands."

"But I am barefoot," wailed Annette, "and I am afraid of the fiddlers."

Fiddler crabs, you know, are n't pleasant things to be dangling around

one's bare feet, and they are more
numerous than sand fleas down at
Henderson's Point.

"True," assented the fisherman;
"then we shall have to wade back."

The fishing was over when they
rounded the point and came in sight
of the cheery bonfire with its Rembrandt-
like group, and the air was savoury with
the smell of frying fish and crabs. The
fisherman was not to be tempted by
appeals to stay, but smilingly disappeared down the sands, the red glare
of his torch making a glowing track in
the water.

"Ah, Mees Annette," whispered Natalie, between mouthfuls of a rich croaker,
"you have found a beau in the water."

"And the fisherman of the Pass, too,"
laughed her cousin Ida.

Annette tossed her head, for Philip
had growled audibly.

"Do you know, Philip," cried

Annette a few days after, rudely shaking him from his siesta on the gallery, — "do you know that I have found my fisherman's hut?"

"Hum," was the only response.

"Yes, and it's the quaintest, most delightful spot imaginable. Philip, do come with me and see it."

"Hum."

"Oh, Philip, you are so lazy; do come with me."

"Yes, but, my dear Annette," protested Philip, "this is a warm day, and I am tired."

Still, his curiosity being aroused, he went grumbling. It was not a very long drive, back from the beach across the railroad and through the pine forest to the bank of a dark, slow-flowing bayou. The fisherman's hut was small, two-roomed, whitewashed, pine-boarded, with the traditional mud chimney acting as a sort of support to one of its uneven sides. Within was a weird assortment of curios from every uncivilized part of the globe. Also were there fishing-tackle and guns in reckless profusion. The fisherman, in the kitchen of the mud-chimney, was sardonically waging war with a basket of little bayou crabs.

"Entrez, mademoiselle et monsieur," he said pleasantly, grabbing a vicious crab by its flippers, and smiling at its wild attempts to bite. "You see I am busy, but make yourself at home."

"Well, how on earth — " began Philip.

"Sh — sh — " whispered Annette. "I was driving out in the woods this morning, and stumbled on the hut. He asked me in, but I came right over after you."

The fisherman, having succeeded in getting the last crab in the kettle of

4

boiling water, came forward smiling and began to explain the curios.

"Then you have not always lived at Pass Christian," said Philip.

"Mais non, monsieur, I am spending a summer here."

"And he spends his winters, doubtless, selling fish in the French market," spitefully soliloquised Philip.

The fisherman was looking unutterable things into Annette's eyes, and, it seemed to Philip, taking an unconscionably long time explaining the use of an East Indian stiletto.

"Oh, would n't it be delightful!" came from Annette at last.

"What?" asked Philip.

"Why, Monsieur LeConte says he'll take six of us out in his catboat tomorrow for a fishing-trip on the Gulf."

"Hum," drily.

"And I'll get Natalie and her cousins."

"Yes," still more drily.

Annette chattered on, entirely oblivious of the strainedness of the men's adieux, and still chattered as they drove through the pines.

"I did not know that you were going to take fishermen and marchands into the bosom of your social set when you came here," growled Philip, at last.

"But, Cousin Phil, can't you see he is a gentleman? The fact that he makes no excuses or protestations is a proof."

"You are a fool," was the polite response.

Still, at six o'clock next morning, there was a little crowd of seven upon the pier, laughing and chatting at the little "Virginie" dipping her bows in the water and flapping her sails in the brisk wind. Natalie's pink bonnet blushed in the early sunshine, and Natalie's

mamma, comely and portly, did chaper-
onage duty. It was not long before
the sails gave swell into the breeze and
the little boat scurried to the Sound.
Past the lighthouse on its gawky iron
stalls, she flew, and now rounded the
white sands of Cat Island.

" Bravo, the Gulf! " sang a voice on
the lookout. The little boat dipped,
halted an instant, then rushed fast into
the blue Gulf waters.

" We will anchor here," said the host,
" have luncheon, and fish."

Philip could not exactly understand
why the fisherman should sit so close
to Annette and whisper so much into
her ears. He chafed at her acting the
part of hostess, and was possessed of a
murderous desire to throw the pink
sun-bonnet and its owner into the sea,
when Natalie whispered audibly to one
of her cousins that " Mees Annette act
nice wit' her lovare."

The sun was banking up flaming pillars of rose and gold in the west when the little "Virginie" rounded Cat Island on her way home, and the quick Southern twilight was fast dying into darkness when she was tied up to the pier and the merry-makers sprang off with baskets of fish. Annette had distinguished herself by catching one small shark, and had immediately ceased to fish and devoted her attention to her fisherman and his line. Philip had angled fiercely, landing trout, croakers, sheepshead, snappers in bewildering luck. He had broken each hopeless captive's neck savagely, as though they were personal enemies. He did not look happy as they landed, though pæans of praise were being sung in his honour.

As the days passed on, " the fisherman of the Pass " began to dance attendance on Annette. What had

seemed a joke became serious. Aunt
Nina, urged by Philip, remonstrated,
and even the mamma of the pink sun-
bonnet began to look grave. It was
all very well for a city demoiselle to
talk with a fisherman and accept favours
at his hands, provided that the city
demoiselle understood that a vast and
bridgeless gulf stretched between her
and the fisherman. But when the
demoiselle forgot the gulf and the
fisherman refused to recognise it, why,
it was time to take matters in hand.

To all of Aunt Nina's remonstran-
ces, Philip's growlings, and the averted
glances of her companions, Annette
was deaf. "You are narrow-minded,"
she said laughingly. "I am interested
in Monsieur LeConte simply as a
study. He is entertaining; he talks
well of his travels, and as for refusing to
recognise the difference between us, why,
he never dreamed of such a thing."

Suddenly a peremptory summons home from Annette's father put an end to the fears of Philip. Annette pouted, but papa must be obeyed. She blamed Philip and Aunt Nina for telling tales, but Aunt Nina was uncommunicative, and Philip too obviously cheerful to derive much satisfaction from.

That night she walked with the fisherman hand in hand on the sands. The wind from the pines bore the scarcely recognisable, subtle freshness of early autumn, and the waters had a hint of dying summer in their sob on the beach.

" You will remember," said the fisherman, " that I have told you nothing about myself."

" Yes," murmured Annette.

" And you will keep your promises to me ? "

" Yes."

" Let me hear you repeat them again."

"I promise you that I will not forget you. I promise you that I will never speak of you to anyone until I see you again. I promise that I will then clasp your hand wherever you may be."

"And mademoiselle will not be discouraged, but will continue her studies?"

"Yes."

It was all very romantic, by the waves of the Sound, under a harvest moon, that seemed all sympathy for these two, despite the fact that it was probably looking down upon hundreds of other equally romantic couples. Annette went to bed with glowing cheeks, and a heart whose pulsations would have caused a physician to prescribe unlimited digitalis.

It was still hot in New Orleans when she returned home, and it seemed hard to go immediately to work But if one is going to be an opera-singer some

day and capture the world with one's
voice, there is nothing to do but to
study, study, sing, practise, even though
one's throat be parched, one's head a
great ache, and one's heart a nest of
discouragement and sadness at what
seems the uselessness of it all. Annette
had now a new incentive to work; the
fisherman had once praised her voice
when she hummed a barcarole on the
sands, and he had insisted that there was
power in its rich notes. Though the
fisherman had showed no cause why he
should be accepted as a musical critic,
Annette had somehow respected his
judgment and been accordingly elated.

It was the night of the opening of
the opera. There was the usual crush,
the glitter and confusing radiance of
the brilliant audience. Annette, with
papa, Aunt Nina, and Philip, was late
reaching her box. The curtain was

up, and " La Juive" was pouring forth
defiance at her angry persecutors.
Annette listened breathlessly.   In
fancy, she too was ringing her voice
out to an applauding house.   Her
head unconsciously beat time to the
music, and one hand half held her
cloak from her bare shoulders.

Then Eleazar appeared, and the
house rose at the end of his song.
Encores it gave, and bravos and cheers.
He bowed calmly, swept his eyes over
the tiers until they found Annette,
where they rested in a half-smile of
recognition.

" Philip," gasped Annette, nervously
raising her glasses, " my fisherman ! "

" Yes, an opera-singer is better than
a marchand," drawled Philip.

The curtain fell on the first act.
The house was won by the new tenor;
it called and recalled him before the
curtain.   Clearly he had sung his way

into the hearts of his audience at once.

" Papa, Aunt Nina," said Annette, " you must come behind the scenes with me. I want you to meet him. He is delightful. You must come."

Philip was bending ostentatiously over the girl in the next box. Papa and Aunt Nina consented to be dragged behind the scenes. Annette was well known, for, in hopes of some day being an occupant of one of the dressing-rooms, she had made friends with everyone connected with the opera.

Eleazar received them, still wearing his brown garb and patriarchal beard.

" How you deceived me ! " she laughed, when the greetings and introductions were over.

" I came to America early," he smiled back at her, " and thought I 'd try a little incognito at the Pass. I was not well, you see.   It has been of great benefit to me."

"I kept my promise," she said in a lower tone.

"Thank you; that also has helped me."

Annette's teacher began to note a wonderful improvement in his pupil's voice.   Never did a girl study so hard or practise so faithfully.   It was truly wonderful.   Now and then Annette would say to papa as if to reassure herself, —

"And when Monsieur Cherbart says I am ready to go to Paris, I may go, papa?"

And papa would say a "Certainly" that would send her back to the piano with renewed ardour.

As for Monsieur LeConte, he was the idol of New Orleans.   Seldom had there been a tenor who had sung himself so completely into the very hearts

of a populace. When he was billed,
the opera displayed " Standing Room "
signs, no matter what the other attrac-
tions in the city might be. Sometimes
Monsieur LeConte delighted small
audiences in Annette's parlour, when
the hostess was in a perfect flutter of
happiness. Not often, you know, for
the leading tenor was in great demand
at the homes of society queens.

" Do you know," said Annette, petulantly, one evening, " I wish for the old
days at Pass Christian."

" So do I," he answered tenderly ;
" will you repeat them with me next
summer ? "

" If I only could ! " she gasped.

Still she might have been happy, had
it not been for Madame Dubeau, —
Madame Dubeau, the flute-voiced leading soprano, who wore the single dainty
curl on her forehead, and thrilled her
audiences oftentimes more completely

than the fisherman. Madame Dubeau
was La Juive to his Eleazar, Leonore
to his Manfred, Elsa to his Lohengrin,
Aida to his Rhadames, Marguerite to
his Faust; in brief, Madame Dubeau
was his opposite. She caressed him as
Mignon, pleaded with him as Michaela,
died for him in " Les Huguenots," broke
her heart for love of him in " La Favo-
rite." How could he help but love
her, Annette asked herself, how could
he? Madame Dubeau was beautiful
and gifted and charming.

Once she whispered her fears to him
when there was the meagrest bit of an
opportunity. He laughed. "You don't
understand, little one," he said tenderly; "the relations of professional
people to each other are peculiar. After
you go to Paris, you will know."

Still, New Orleans had built up its
romance, and gossiped accordingly.

" Have you heard the news? " whis-

pered Lola to Annette, leaning from
her box at the opera one night. The
curtain had just gone up on " Hero-
dias," and for some reason or other,
the audience applauded with more
warmth than usual. There was a
noticeable number of good-humoured,
benignant smiles on the faces of the
applauders.

"No," answered Annette, breathlessly,— " no, indeed, Lola ; I am going
to Paris next week. I am so delighted
I can't stop to think."

"Yes, that is excellent," said Lola,
" but all New Orleans is smiling at
the romance. Monsieur LeConte and
Madame Dubeau were quietly married
last night, but it leaked out this afternoon. See all the applause she's
receiving ! "

Annette leaned back in her chair,
very white and still. Her box was
empty after the first act, and a quiet

little tired voice that was almost too
faint to be heard in the carriage on the
way home, said —

"Papa, I don't think I care to go
to Paris, after all."

M'SIEU FORTIER'S VIOLIN

5

M'SIEU FORTIER'S VIOLIN

SLOWLY, one by one, the lights in the French Opera go out, until there is but a single glimmer of pale yellow flickering in the great dark space, a few moments ago all a-glitter with jewels and the radiance of womanhood and a-clash with music. Darkness now, and silence, and a great haunted hush over all, save for the distant cheery voice of a stage hand humming a bar of the opera.

The glimmer of gas makes a halo about the bowed white head of a little old man putting his violin carefully away in its case with aged, trembling, nervous fingers. Old M'sieu Fortier was the last one out every night.

Outside the air was murky, foggy. Gas and electricity were but faint

splotches of light on the thick curtain
of fog and mist.   Around the opera
was a mighty bustle of carriages and
drivers and footmen, with a car gaining
headway in the street now and then, a
howling of names and numbers, the
laughter and small talk of cloaked society stepping slowly to its carriages, and
the more bourgeoisie vocalisation of the
foot passengers who streamed along and
hummed little bits of music.   The fog's
denseness was confusing, too, and at one
moment it seemed that the little narrow
street would become inextricably choked
and remain so until some mighty engine
would blow the crowd into atoms.   It
had been a crowded night.   From
around Toulouse Street, where led the
entrance to the troisièmes, from the
grand stairway, from the entrance to
the quatrièmes, the human stream
poured into the street, nearly all with
a song on their lips.

M'sieu Fortier stood at the corner, blinking at the beautiful ladies in their carriages. He exchanged a hearty salutation with the saloon-keeper at the corner, then, tenderly carrying his violin case, he trudged down Bourbon Street, a little old, bent, withered figure, with shoulders shrugged up to keep warm, as though the faded brown overcoat were not thick enough.

Down on Bayou Road, not so far from Claiborne Street, was a house, little and old and queer, but quite large enough to hold M'sieu Fortier, a wrinkled dame, and a white cat. He was home but little, for on nearly every day there were rehearsals; then on Tuesday, Thursday, and Saturday nights, and twice Sundays there were performances, so Ma'am Jeanne and the white cat kept house almost always alone. Then, when M'sieu Fortier was at home, why, it was practice, practice all the day, and smoke, snore, sleep at night. Altogether it was not very exhilarating.

M'sieu Fortier had played first violin in the orchestra ever since — well, no one remembered his not playing there. Sometimes there would come breaks in the seasons, and for a year the great building would be dark and silent. Then M'sieu Fortier would do jobs of playing here and there, one night for this ball, another night for that soirée dansante, and in the day, work at his trade, — that of a cigar-maker. But now for seven years there had been no break in the season, and the little old violinist was happy. There is nothing sweeter than a regular job and good music to play, music into which one can put some soul, some expression, and which one must study to understand. Dance music, of the frivolous, frothy kind deemed essential to soirées, is trivial, easy, uninteresting.

So M'sieu Fortier, Ma'am Jeanne,
and the white cat lived a peaceful, un-
eventful existence out on Bayou Road.
When the opera season was over in
February, M'sieu went back to cigar-
making, and the white cat purred none
the less contentedly.

It had been a benefit to-night for
the leading tenor, and he had chosen
" Roland à Ronceveaux," a favourite
this season, for his farewell.   And, mon
Dieu, mused the little M'sieu, but how
his voice had rung out bell-like, piercing
above the chorus of the first act !   Encore after encore was given, and the
bravos of the troisièmes were enough
to stir the most sluggish of pulses.

> " Superbes Pyrenées
> Qui dressez dans le ciel,
> Vos cimes couronnées
> D'un hiver éternelle,
> Pour nous livrer passage
> Ouvrez vos larges flancs,
> Faîtes taire l'orage,
> Voici, venir les Francs ! "

M'sieu quickened his pace down
Bourbon Street as he sang the chorus
to himself in a thin old voice, and then,
before he could see in the thick fog,
he had run into two young men.

"I — I — beg your pardon, — mes-
sieurs," he stammered.

"Most certainly," was the careless
response; then the speaker, taking a
second glance at the object of the ren-
contre, cried joyfully :

"Oh, M'sieu Fortier, is it you?
Why, you are so happy, singing your
love sonnet to your-lady's eyebrow, that
you did n't see a thing but the moon,
did you? And who is the fair one
who should clog your senses so?"

There was a deprecating shrug from
the little man.

"Ma foi, but monsieur must know
fo' sho', dat I am too old for love
songs!"

"I know nothing save that I want

that violin of yours.   When is it to be mine, M'sieu Fortier?"

"Nevare, nevare!" exclaimed M'sieu, gripping on as tightly to the case as if he feared it might be wrenched from him.   "Me a lovere, and to sell mon violon!   Ah, so ver' foolish!"

"Martel," said the first speaker to his companion as they moved on up town, "I wish you knew that little Frenchman.   He's a unique specimen. He has the most exquisite violin I 've seen in years; beautiful and mellow as a genuine Cremona, and he can make the music leap, sing, laugh, sob, skip, wail, anything you like from under his bow when he wishes.   It's something wonderful.   We are good friends. Picked him up in my French-town rambles.   I 've been trying to buy that instrument since —"

"To throw it aside a week later?" lazily inquired Martel.   "You are like the rest of these nineteenth-century vandals, you can see nothing picturesque that you do not wish to deface for a souvenir; you cannot even let simple happiness alone, but must needs destroy it in a vain attempt to make it your own or parade it as an advertisement."

As for M'sieu Fortier, he went right on with his song and turned into Bayou Road, his shoulders still shrugged high as though he were cold, and into the quaint little house, where Ma'am Jeanne and the white cat, who always waited up for him at nights, were both nodding over the fire.

It was not long after this that the opera closed, and M'sieu went back to his old out-of-season job. But somehow he did not do as well this spring and summer as always. There is a certain amount of cunning and finesse required to roll a cigar just so, that

M'sieu seemed to be losing, whether from age or deterioration it was hard to tell. Nevertheless, there was just about half as much money coming in as formerly, and the quaint little pucker between M'sieu's eyebrows which served for a frown came oftener and stayed longer than ever before.

"Minesse," he said one day to the white cat, — he told all his troubles to her; it was of no use to talk to Ma'am Jeanne, she was too deaf to understand, — "Minesse, we are gettin' po'. You' père git h'old, an' hees han's dey go no mo' rapidement, an' dere be no mo' soirées dese day. Minesse, eef la saison don' hurry up, we shall eat ver' lil' meat."

And Minesse curled her tail and purred.

Before the summer had fairly begun, strange rumours began to float about in musical circles. M. Maugé would no longer manage the opera, but it would be turned into the hands of Americans, a syndicate. Bah! These English-speaking people could do nothing unless there was a trust, a syndicate, a company immense and dishonest. It was going to be a guarantee business, with a strictly financial basis. But worse than all this, the new manager, who was now in France, would not only procure the artists, but a new orchestra, a new leader. M'sieu Fortier grew apprehensive at this, for he knew what the loss of his place would mean to him.

September and October came, and the papers were filled with accounts of the new artists from France and of the new orchestra leader too. He was described as a most talented, progressive, energetic young man. M'sieu Fortier's heart sank at the word " progressive." He was anything but that.

The New Orleans Creole blood flowed too sluggishly in his old veins.

November came; the opera reopened. M'sieu Fortier was not re-engaged.

"Minesse," he said with a catch in his voice that strongly resembled a sob, "Minesse, we mus' go hongry sometime. Ah, mon pauvre violon! Ah, mon Dieu, dey put us h'out, an' dey will not have us. Nev' min', we will sing anyhow." And drawing his bow across the strings, he sang in his thin, quavering voice, "Salut demeure, chaste et pure."

It is strange what a peculiar power of fascination former haunts have for the human mind. The criminal, after he has fled from justice, steals back and skulks about the scene of his crime; the employee thrown from work hangs about the place of his former industry; the schoolboy, truant or expelled, peeps in at the school-gate and

taunts the good boys within. M'sieu
Fortier was no exception. Night after
night of the performances he climbed
the stairs of the opera and sat, an atten-
tive listener to the orchestra, with one
ear inclined to the stage, and a quizzi-
cal expression on his wrinkled face.
Then he would go home, and pat
Minesse, and fondle the violin.

"Ah, Minesse, dose new player!
Not one bit can dey play. Such tones,
Minesse, such tones! All the time
portemento, oh, so ver' bad! Ah, mon
chere violon, we can play." And he
would play and sing a romance, and
smile tenderly to himself.

At first it used to be into the deuxièmes that M'sieu Fortier went, into
the front seats. But soon they were
too expensive, and after all, one could
hear just as well in the fourth row as in
the first. After a while even the rear
row of the deuxièmes was too costly,

and the little musician wended his way
with the plebeians around on Toulouse
Street, and climbed the long, tedious
flight of stairs into the troisièmes.   It
makes no difference to be one row
higher.   It was more to the liking, after
all.   One felt more at home up here
among the people.   If one was thirsty,
one could drink a glass of wine or beer
being passed about by the libretto boys,
and the music sounded just as well.

But it happened one night that
M'sieu could not even afford to climb
the Toulouse Street stairs.   To be sure,
there was yet another gallery, the quatrièmes, where the peanut boys went for a
dime, but M'sieu could not get down to
that yet.   So he stayed outside until all
the beautiful women in their warm
wraps, a bright-hued chattering throng,
came down the grand staircase to their
carriages.

It was on one of these nights that

Courcey and Martel found him shivering at the corner.

"Hello, M'sieu Fortier," cried Courcey, "are you ready to let me have that violin yet?"

"For shame!" interrupted Martel.

"Fifty dollars, you know," continued Courcey, taking no heed of his friend's interpolation.

M'sieu Fortier made a courtly bow. "Eef Monsieur will call at my 'ouse on de morrow, he may have mon violon," he said huskily; then turned abruptly on his heel, and went down Bourbon Street, his shoulders drawn high as though he were cold.

When Courcey and Martel entered the gate of the little house on Bayou Road the next day, there floated out to their ears a wordless song thrilling from the violin, a song that told more than speech or tears or gestures could have done of the utter sorrow and desolation of the little old man.   They walked softly up the short red brick walk and tapped at the door.   Within, M'sieu Fortier was caressing the violin, with silent tears streaming down his wrinkled gray face.

There was not much said on either side.   Courcey came away with the instrument, leaving the money behind, while Martel grumbled at the essentially sordid, mercenary spirit of the world. M'sieu Fortier turned back into the room, after bowing his visitors out with old-time French courtliness, and turning to the sleepy white cat, said with a dry sob:

" Minesse, dere's only me an' you now."

About six days later, Courcey's morning dreams were disturbed by the announcement of a visitor.   Hastily doing a toilet, he descended the stairs to find M'sieu Fortier nervously pacing the hall floor.

"I come fo' bring back you' money, yaas. I cannot sleep, I cannot eat, I only cry, and t'ink, and weesh fo' mon violon; and Minesse, an' de ol' woman too, dey mope an' look bad too, all for mon violon. I try fo' to use dat money, but eet burn an' sting lak blood money. I feel lak' I done sol' my child. I cannot go at l'opera no mo', I t'ink of mon violon. I starve befo' I live widout. My heart, he is broke, I die for mon violon."

Courcey left the room and returned with the instrument.

"M'sieu Fortier," he said, bowing low, as he handed the case to the little man, "take your violin; it was a whim with me, a passion with you. And as for the money, why, keep that too; it was worth a hundred dollars to have possessed such an instrument even for six days."

BY THE BAYOU ST. JOHN

BY THE BAYOU ST. JOHN

THE Bayou St. John slowly makes its dark-hued way through reeds and rushes, high banks and flat slopes, until it casts itself into the turbulent bosom of Lake Pontchartrain. It is dark, like the passionate women of Egypt; placid, like their broad brows; deep, silent, like their souls. Within its bosom are hidden romances and stories, such as were sung by minstrels of old. From the source to the mouth is not far distant, visibly speaking, but in the life of the bayou a hundred heart-miles could scarce measure it. Just where it winds about the northwest of the city are some of its most beautiful bits, orange groves on one side, and quaint old Spanish gardens on the other.

Who cares that the bridges are modern, and that here and there pert boat-houses rear their prim heads? It is the bayou, even though it be invaded with the ruthless vandalism of the improving idea, and can a boat-house kill the beauty of a moss-grown centurion of an oak with a history as old as the city? Can an iron bridge with tarantula piers detract from the song of a mocking-bird in a fragrant orange grove? We know that farther out, past the Confederate Soldiers' Home, — that rose-embowered, rambling place of gray-coated, white-haired old men with broken hearts for a lost cause, — it flows, unimpeded by the faintest conception of man, and we love it all the more that, like the Priestess of Isis, it is calm-browed, even in indignity.

To its banks at the end of Moss Street, one day there came a man and a maiden. They were both tall and lithe and slender, with the agility of youth and fire. He was the final concentration of the essence of Spanish passion filtered into an American frame ; she, a repressed Southern exotic, trying to fit itself into the niches of a modern civilisation. Truly, a fitting couple to seek the bayou banks.

They climbed the levee that stretched a feeble check to waters that seldom rise, and on the other side of the embankment, at the brink of the river, she sat on a log, and impatiently pulled off the little cap she wore. The skies were gray, heavy, overcast, with an occasional wind-rift in the clouds that only revealed new depths of grayness behind ; the tideless waters murmured a faint ripple against the logs and jutting beams of the breakwater, and were answered by the crescendo wail of the dried reeds on the other bank, — reeds that rustled and moaned among themselves for the golden days of summer sunshine.

He stood up, his dark form a slender silhouette against the sky; she looked upward from her log, and their eyes met with an exquisite shock of recognising understanding; dark eyes into dark eyes, Iberian fire into Iberian fire, soul unto soul: it was enough. He sat down and took her into his arms, and in the eerie murmur of the storm coming they talked of the future.

"And then I hope to go to Italy or France. It is only there, beneath those far Southern skies, that I could ever hope to attain to anything that the soul within me says I can. I have wasted so much time in the mere struggle for bread, while the powers of a higher calling have clamoured for recognition and expression. I will go some day and redeem myself."

She was silent a moment, watching

with half-closed lids a dejected-looking hunter on the other bank, and a lean dog who trailed through the reeds behind him with drooping tail.   Then she asked:

"And I — what will become of me?"

"You, Athanasia?   There is a great future before you, little woman, and I and my love can only mar it.   Try to forget me and go your way.   I am only the epitome of unhappiness and ill-success."

But she laughed and would have none of it.

Will you ever forget that day, Athanasia?   How the little gamins, Creole throughout, came half shyly near the log, fishing, and exchanging furtive whispers and half-concealed glances at the silent couple.   Their angling was rewarded only by a little black water-moccasin that wriggled and forked its venomous red tongue in an attempt to exercise its death-dealing prerogative. This Athanasia insisted must go back into its native black waters, and paid the price the boys asked that it might enjoy its freedom. The gamins laughed and chattered in their soft patois; the Don smiled tenderly upon Athanasia, and she durst not look at the reeds as she talked, lest their crescendo sadness yield a foreboding. Just then a wee girl appeared, clad in a multi-hued garment, evidently a sister to the small fishermen. Her keen black eyes set in a dusky face glanced sharply and suspiciously at the group as she clambered over the wet embankment, and it seemed the drizzling mist grew colder, the sobbing wind more pronounced in its prophetic wail. Athanasia rose suddenly. " Let us go," she said; " the eternal feminine has spoiled it all."

The bayou flows as calmly, as darkly, as full of hidden passions as ever. On

a night years after, the moon was shining upon it with a silvery tenderness
that seemed brighter, more caressingly
lingering than anywhere within the old
city.　Behind, there rose the spires and
towers; before, only the reeds, green
now, and soft in their rustlings and
whisperings for the future.　False reeds!
They tell themselves of their happiness
to be, and it all ends in dry stalks and
drizzling skies.　The mocking-bird in
the fragrant orange grove sends out his
night song, and blends it with the
cricket's chirp, as the blossoms of
orange and magnolia mingle their perfume with the earthy smell of a summer
rain just blown over.　Perfect in its
stillness, absolute in its beauty, tenderly
healing in its suggestion of peace, the
night in its clear-lighted, cloudless sweet-
ness enfolds Athanasia, as she stands on
the levee and gazes down at the old log,
now almost hidden in the luxuriant grass.

" It was the eternal feminine that spoiled our dream that day as it spoiled the after life, was it not ? "

But the Bayou St. John did not answer.   It merely gathered into its silent bosom another broken-hearted romance, and flowed dispassionately on its way.

WHEN THE BAYOU
OVERFLOWS

WHEN THE BAYOU
OVERFLOWS

WHEN the sun goes down behind the great oaks along the Bayou Teche near Franklin, it throws red needles of light into the dark woods, and leaves a great glow on the still bayou. Ma'am Mouton paused at her gate and cast a contemplative look at the red sky.

"Hit will rain to-morrow, sho'. I mus' git in my t'ings."

Ma'am Mouton's remark must have been addressed to herself or to the lean dog, for no one else was visible. She moved briskly about the yard, taking things from the line, when Louisette's voice called cheerily:

"Ah, Ma'am Mouton, can I help?"

Louisette was petite and plump and

black-haired.   Louisette's eyes danced, and her lips were red and tempting. Ma'am Mouton's face relaxed as the small brown hands relieved hers of their burden.

"Sylves', has he come yet?" asked the red mouth.

"Mais non, ma chère," said Ma'am Mouton, sadly, "I can' tell fo' w'y he no come home soon dese day. Ah me, I feel lak' somet'ing goin' happen. He so strange."

Even as she spoke a quick nervous step was heard crunching up the brick walk.   Sylves' paused an instant without the kitchen door, his face turned to the setting sun.   He was tall and slim and agile; a true 'cajan.

"Bon jour, Louisette," he laughed. "Eh, maman!"

"Ah, my son, you are ver' late."

Sylves' frowned, but said nothing. It was a silent supper that followed.

Louisette was sad, Ma'am Mouton
sighed now and then, Sylves' was
constrained.

"Maman," he said at length, "I am
goin' away."

Ma'am Mouton dropped her fork
and stared at him with unseeing eyes;
then, as she comprehended his remark,
she put her hand out to him with a
pitiful gesture.

"Sylves'!" cried Louisette, spring-
ing to her feet.

"Maman, don't, don't!" he said
weakly; then gathering strength from
the silence, he burst forth:

"Yaas, I 'm goin' away to work.
I 'm tired of dis, jus' dig, dig, work
in de fiel', nothin' to see but de cloud,
de tree, de bayou. I don't lak' New
Orleans; it too near here, dere no mo'
money dere. I go up fo' Mardi Gras,
an' de same people, de same strit'.
I 'm goin' to Chicago!"

7

"Sylves'!" screamed both women at once.

Chicago! That vast, far-off city that seemed in another world. Chicago! A name to conjure with for wickedness.

"W'y, yaas," continued Sylves', "lots of boys I know dere. Henri an' Joseph Lascaud an' Arthur, dey write me what money dey mek' in cigar. I can mek' a livin' too. I can mek' fine cigar. See how I do in New Orleans in de winter."

"Oh, Sylves'," wailed Louisette, "den you'll forget me!"

"Non, non, ma chère," he answered tenderly. "I will come back when the bayou overflows again, an' maman an' Louisette will have fine present."

Ma'am Mouton had bowed her head on her hands, and was rocking to and fro in an agony of dry-eyed misery.

Sylves' went to her side and knelt. "Maman," he said softly, "maman,

you mus' not cry. All de boys go
'way, an' I will come back reech, an'
you won't have fo' to work no mo'."

But Ma'am Mouton was incon-
solable.

It was even as Sylves' had said.
In the summer-time the boys of the
Bayou Teche would work in the field
or in the town of Franklin, hack-driv-
ing and doing odd jobs. When winter
came, there was a general exodus to
New Orleans, a hundred miles away,
where work was to be had as cigar-
makers. There is money, plenty of it,
in cigar-making, if one can get in the
right place. Of late, however, there
had been a general slackness of the
trade. Last winter oftentimes Sylves'
had walked the streets out of work.
Many were the Creole boys who had
gone to Chicago to earn a living, for
the cigar-making trade flourishes there
wonderfully. Friends of Sylves' had

gone, and written home glowing accounts of the money to be had almost for the asking.   When one's blood leaps for new scenes, new adventures, and one needs money, what is the use of frittering away time alternately between the Bayou Teche and New Orleans? Sylves' had brooded all summer, and now that September had come, he was determined to go.

Louisette, the orphan, the girl-lover, whom everyone in Franklin knew would some day be Ma'am Mouton's daughter-in-law, wept and pleaded in vain.   Sylves' kissed her quivering lips.

" Ma chère," he would say, " t'ink, I will bring you one fine diamon' ring, nex' spring, when de bayou overflows again."

Louisette would fain be content with this promise.   As for Ma'am Mouton, she seemed to have grown ages older.

Her Sylves' was going from her; Sylves', whose trips to New Orleans had been a yearly source of heart-break, was going far away for months to that mistily wicked city, a thousand miles away.

October came, and Sylves' had gone. Ma'am Mouton had kept up bravely until the last, when with one final cry she extended her arms to the pitiless train bearing him northward. Then she and Louisette went home drearily, the one leaning upon the other.

Ah, that was a great day when the first letter came from Chicago! Louisette came running in breathlessly from the post-office, and together they read it again and again. Chicago was such a wonderful city, said Sylves'. Why, it was always like New Orleans at Mardi Gras with the people. He had seen Joseph Lascaud, and he had a place to work promised him. He was

well, but he wanted, oh, so much, to
see maman and Louisette. But then,
he could wait.

Was ever such a wonderful letter?
Louisette sat for an hour afterwards
building gorgeous air-castles, while
Ma'am Mouton fingered the paper
and murmured prayers to the Virgin
for Sylves'. When the bayou overflowed again? That would be in April.
Then Louisette caught herself looking
critically at her slender brown fingers,
and blushed furiously, though Ma'am
Mouton could not see her in the
gathering twilight.

Next week there was another letter,
even more wonderful than the first.
Sylves' had found work. He was making cigars, and was earning two dollars
a day. Such wages! Ma'am Mouton
and Louisette began to plan pretty
things for the brown cottage on the
Teche.

That was a pleasant winter, after all. True, there was no Sylves', but then he was always in New Orleans for a few months any way. There were his letters, full of wondrous tales of the great queer city, where cars went by ropes underground, and where there was no Mardi Gras and the people did not mind Lent. Now and then there would be a present, a keepsake for Louisette, and some money for maman. They would plan improvements for the cottage, and Louisette began to do sewing and dainty crochet, which she would hide with a blush if anyone hinted at a trousseau.

It was March now, and Spring-time. The bayou began to sweep down between its banks less sluggishly than before; it was rising, and soon would spread over its tiny levees. The doors could be left open now, though the trees were not yet green; but then

down here the trees do not swell and
bud slowly and tease you for weeks
with promises of greenness. Dear no,
they simply look mysterious, and their
twigs shake against each other and tell
secrets of the leaves that will soon be
born. Then one morning you awake,
and lo, it is a green world! The
boughs have suddenly clothed themselves all in a wondrous garment, and
you feel the blood run riot in your
veins out of pure sympathy.

One day in March, it was warm and
sweet. Underfoot were violets, and
wee white star flowers peering through
the baby-grass. The sky was blue,
with flecks of white clouds reflecting
themselves in the brown bayou.
Louisette tripped up the red brick
walk with the Chicago letter in her
hand, and paused a minute at the door
to look upon the leaping waters, her
eyes dancing.

"I know the bayou must be ready to overflow," went the letter in the carefully phrased French that the brothers taught at the parochial school, "and I am glad, for I want to see the dear maman and my Louisette. I am not so well, and Monsieur le docteur says it is well for me to go to the South again."

Monsieur le docteur! Sylves' not well! The thought struck a chill to the hearts of Ma'am Mouton and Louisette, but not for long. Of course, Sylves' was not well, he needed some of maman's tisanes. Then he was homesick; it was to be expected.

At last the great day came, Sylves' would be home. The brown waters of the bayou had spread until they were seemingly trying to rival the Mississippi in width. The little house was scrubbed and cleaned until it shone again. Louisette had looked her dainty little dress over and over to be sure that there was not a flaw to be found wherein Sylves' could compare her unfavourably to the stylish Chicago girls.

The train rumbled in on the platform, and two pair of eyes opened wide for the first glimpse of Sylves'. The porter, all officiousness and brass buttons, bustled up to Ma'am Mouton.

"This is Mrs. Mouton?" he inquired deferentially.

Ma'am Mouton nodded, her heart sinking. "Where is Sylves'?"

"He is here, madam."

There appeared Joseph Lascaud, then some men bearing Something. Louisette put her hands up to her eyes to hide the sight, but Ma'am Mouton was rigid.

"It was too cold for him," Joseph was saying to almost deaf ears, "and he took the consumption. He thought

he could get well when he come home.
He talk all the way down about the
bayou, and about you and Louisette.
Just three hours ago he had a bad
hemorrhage, and he died from weakness. Just three hours ago. He said
he wanted to get home and give Louisette her diamond ring, when the
bayou overflowed."

MR. BAPTISTE

MR. BAPTISTE

HE might have had another name; we never knew. Some one had christened him Mr. Baptiste long ago in the dim past, and it sufficed. No one had ever been known who had the temerity to ask him for another cognomen, for though he was a mild-mannered little man, he had an uncomfortable way of shutting up oyster-wise and looking disagreeable when approached concerning his personal history.

He was small: most Creole men are small when they are old. It is strange, but a fact. It must be that age withers them sooner and more effectually than those of un-Latinised extraction. Mr. Baptiste was, furthermore, very much wrinkled and lame. Like the Son of

Man, he had nowhere to lay his head, save when some kindly family made room for him in a garret or a barn. He subsisted by doing odd jobs, white-washing, cleaning yards, doing errands, and the like.

The little old man was a frequenter of the levee. Never a day passed that his quaint little figure was not seen moving up and down about the ships. Chiefly did he haunt the Texas and Pacific warehouses and the landing-place of the Morgan-line steamships. This seemed like madness, for these spots are almost the busiest on the levee, and the rough seamen and 'longshoremen have least time to be bothered with small weak folks. Still there was method in the madness of Mr. Baptiste. The Morgan steamships, as every one knows, ply between New Orleans and Central and South American ports, doing the major part of the fruit trade; and many were

the baskets of forgotten fruit that Mr.
Baptiste took away with him unmolested.
Sometimes, you know, bananas and
mangoes and oranges and citrons will
half spoil, particularly if it has been a
bad voyage over the stormy Gulf, and
the officers of the ships will give away
stacks of fruit, too good to go into the
river, too bad to sell to the fruit-dealers.

You could see Mr. Baptiste trudging
up the street with his quaint one-sided
walk, bearing his dilapidated basket on
one shoulder, a nondescript head-cover
pulled over his eyes, whistling cheerily.
Then he would slip in at the back door
of one of his clients with a brisk, —

" Ah, bonjour, madame.   Now here
ees jus' a lil' bit fruit, some bananas.
Perhaps madame would cook some for
Mr. Baptiste? "

And madame, who understood and
knew his ways, would fry him some of
the bananas, and set it before him, a

8

tempting dish, with a bit of madame's bread and meat and coffee thrown in for lagniappe; and Mr. Baptiste would depart, filled and contented, leaving the load of fruit behind as madame's pay. Thus did he eat, and his clients were many, and never too tired or too cross to cook his meals and get their pay in baskets of fruit.

One day he slipped in at Madame Garcia's kitchen door with such a woe-begone air, and slid a small sack of nearly ripe plantains on the table with such a misery-laden sigh, that madame, who was fat and excitable, threw up both hands and cried out:

"Mon Dieu, Mistare Baptiste, fo' w'y you look lak dat? What ees de mattare?"

For answer, Mr. Baptiste shook his head gloomily and sighed again. Madame Garcia moved heavily about the kitchen, putting the plantains in

a cool spot and punctuating her foot-
steps with sundry " Mon Dieux " and
" Misères."

" Dose cotton!" ejaculated Mr. Baptiste, at last.

"Ah, mon Dieu ! " groaned Madame
Garcia, rolling her eyes heavenwards.

" Hit will drive de fruit away ! " he
continued.

" Misère! " said Madame Garcia.

" Hit will."

" Oui, oui," said Madame Garcia.
She had carefully inspected the plantains, and seeing that they were good
and wholesome, was inclined to agree
with anything Mr. Baptiste said.

He grew excited. "Yaas, dose cotton-
yardmans, dose 'longsho'mans, dey go
out on one strik'. Dey t'row down
dey tool an' say dey work no mo' wid
niggers. Les veseaux, dey lay in de
river, no work, no cargo, yaas. Den
de fruit ship, dey can' mak' lan', de

mans, dey t'reaten an' say t'ings. Dey mak' big fight, yaas. Dere no mo' work on de levee, lak dat. Ever'body jus' walk roun' an' say cuss word, yaas ! "

"Oh, mon Dieu, mon Dieu!" groaned Madame Garcia, rocking her guinea-blue-clad self to and fro.

Mr. Baptiste picked up his nondescript head-cover and walked out through the brick-reddened alley, talking excitedly to himself. Madame Garcia called after him to know if he did not want his luncheon, but he shook his head and passed on.

Down on the levee it was even as Mr. Baptiste had said. The 'longshoremen, the cotton-yardmen, and the stevedores had gone out on a strike. The levee lay hot and unsheltered under the glare of a noonday sun. The turgid Mississippi scarce seemed to flow, but gave forth a brazen gleam from its yellow bosom. Great vessels lay against the wharf, silent and un-populated. Excited groups of men clustered here and there among bales of uncompressed cotton, lying about in disorderly profusion. Cargoes of mo-lasses and sugar gave out a sticky sweet smell, and now and then the fierce rays of the sun would kindle tiny blazes in the cotton and splinter-mixed dust underfoot.

Mr. Baptiste wandered in and out among the groups of men, exchanging a friendly salutation here and there. He looked the picture of woe-begone misery.

"Hello, Mr. Baptiste," cried á big, brawny Irishman, " sure an' you look, as if you was about to be hanged."

" Ah, mon Dieu," said Mr. Baptiste, " dose fruit ship be ruined fo' dees strik'."

" Damn the fruit!" cheerily replied

the Irishman, artistically disposing of a mouthful of tobacco juice. " It ain't the fruit we care about, it 's the cotton."

" Hear ! hear ! " cried a dozen lusty comrades.

Mr. Baptiste shook his head and moved sorrowfully away.

" Hey, by howly St. Patrick, here 's that little fruit-eater ! " called the centre of another group of strikers perched on cotton-bales.

" Hello ! Where — " began a second ; but the leader suddenly held up his hand for silence, and the men listened eagerly.

It might not have been a sound, for the levee lay quiet and the mules on the cotton-drays dozed languidly, their ears pitched at varying acute angles. But the practised ears of the men heard a familiar sound stealing up over the heated stillness.

" Oh — ho — ho — humph — humph

— humph — ho — ho — ho — oh — o — o — humph!"

Then the faint rattle of chains, and the steady thump of a machine pounding.

If ever you go on the levee you'll know that sound, the rhythmic song of the stevedores heaving cotton-bales, and the steady thump, thump, of the machine compressing them within the hold of the ship.

Finnegan, the leader, who had held up his hand for silence, uttered an oath.

"Scabs! Men, come on!"

There was no need for a further invitation. The men rose in sullen wrath and went down the levee, the crowd gathering in numbers as it passed along. Mr. Baptiste followed in its wake, now and then sighing a mournful protest which was lost in the roar of the men.

"Scabs!" Finnegan had said; and
the word was passed along, until it
seemed that the half of the second District knew and had risen to investigate.

"Oh — ho — ho — humph — humph
— humph — oh — ho — ho — oh — o
— o — humph!"

The rhythmic chorus sounded nearer,
and the cause manifested itself when the
curve of the levee above the French
Market was passed. There rose a
White Star steamer, insolently settling
itself to the water as each consignment
of cotton bales was compressed into her
hold.

"Niggers!" roared Finnegan wrathily.

"Niggers! niggers! Kill 'em, scabs!"
chorused the crowd.

With muscles standing out like
cables through their blue cotton shirts,
and sweat rolling from glossy black
skins, the Negro stevedores were at work
steadily labouring at the cotton, with the

rhythmic song swinging its cadence in the hot air. The roar of the crowd caused the men to look up with momentary apprehension, but at the overseer's reassuring word they bent back to work.

Finnegan was a Titan. With livid face and bursting veins he ran into the street facing the French Market, and uprooted a huge block of paving stone. Staggering under its weight, he rushed back to the ship, and with one mighty effort hurled it into the hold.

The delicate poles of the costly machine tottered in the air, then fell forward with a crash as the whole iron framework in the hold collapsed.

"Damn ye," shouted Finnegan, "now yez can pack yer cotton!"

The crowd's cheers at this changed to howls, as the Negroes, infuriated at their loss, for those costly machines belong to the labourers and not to the

ship-owners, turned upon the mob and
began to throw brickbats, pieces of
iron, chunks of wood, anything that
cai e to hand. It was pandemonium
turned loose over a turgid stream, with
a malarial sun to heat the passions to
fever point.

Mr. Baptiste had taken refuge behind
a bread-stall on the outside of the market. He had taken off his cap, and
was weakly cheering the Negroes on.

" Bravo ! cheered Mr. Baptiste.

" Will yez look at that damned fruit-
eatin' Frinchman ! " howled McMahon.
" Cheerin' the niggers, are you ? " and
he let fly a brickbat in the direction of
the bread-stall.

" Oh, mon Dieu, mon Dieu ! " wailed
the bread-woman.

Mr. Baptiste lay very still, with a
great ugly gash in his wrinkled brown
temple. Fishmen and vegetable marchands gathered around him in a quick,

sympathetic mass. The individual, the concrete bit of helpless humanity, had more interest for them than the vast, vague fighting mob beyond.

The noon-hour pealed from the brazen throats of many bells, and the numerous hoarse whistles of the steamboats called the unheeded luncheon-time to the levee workers. The war waged furiously, and groans of the wounded mingled with curses and roars from the combatants.

" Killed instantly," said the surgeon, carefully lifting Mr. Baptiste into the ambulance.

Tramp, tramp, tramp, sounded the militia steadily marching down Decatur Street.

" Whist! do yez hear!" shouted Finnegan; and the conflict had ceased ere the yellow river could reflect the sun from the polished bayonets.

You remember, of course, how long

the strike lasted, and how many battles
were fought and lives lost before the
final adjustment of affairs. It was a
fearsome war, and many forgot afterwards whose was the first life lost in
the struggle, — poor little Mr. Baptiste's,
whose body lay at the Morgue un-
claimed for days before it was finally
dropped unnamed into Potter's Field.

A CARNIVAL JANGLE

A CARNIVAL JANGLE

THERE is a merry jangle of bells in the
air, an all-pervading sense of jester's
noise, and the flaunting vividness of
royal colours.   The streets swarm with
humanity, — humanity in all shapes,
manners, forms, laughing, pushing,
jostling, crowding, a mass of men and
women and children, as varied and as-
sorted in their several individual pecu-
liarities as ever a crowd that gathered
in one locality since the days of Babel.

It is Carnival in New Orleans; a
brilliant Tuesday in February, when
the very air gives forth an ozone in-
tensely exhilarating, making one long
to cut capers. The buildings are a
blazing mass of royal purple and golden
yellow, national flags, bunting, and deco-

rations that laugh in the glint of the Midas sun. The streets are a crush of jesters and maskers, Jim Crows and clowns, ballet girls and Mephistos, Indians and monkeys; of wild and sudden flashes of music, of glittering pageants and comic ones, of befeathered and belled horses; a dream of colour and melody and fantasy gone wild in an effervescent bubble of beauty that shifts and changes and passes kaleidoscope-like before the bewildered eye.

A bevy of bright-eyed girls and boys of that uncertain age that hovers between childhood and maturity, were moving down Canal Street when there was a sudden jostle with another crowd meeting them. For a minute there was a deafening clamour of shouts and laughter, cracking of the whips, which all maskers carry, a jingle and clatter of carnival bells, and the masked and un-masked extricated themselves and moved

from each other's paths. But in the
confusion a tall Prince of Darkness had
whispered to one of the girls in the unmasked crowd : " You 'd better come
with us, Flo ; you 're wasting time in
that tame gang. Slip off, they 'll never
miss you ; we 'll get you a rig, and show
you what life is."

And so it happened, when a half-
hour passed, and the bright-eyed bevy
missed Flo and could n't find her, wisely
giving up the search at last, she, the
quietest and most bashful of the lot,
was being initiated into the mysteries
of " what life is."

Down Bourbon Street and on Toulouse and St. Peter Streets there are
quaint little old-world places where one
may be disguised effectually for a tiny
consideration. Thither, guided by the
shapely Mephisto and guarded by the
team of jockeys and ballet girls, tripped
Flo. Into one of the lowest-ceiled,

dingiest, and most ancient-looking of these shops they stepped.

"A disguise for the demoiselle," announced Mephisto to the woman who met them. She was small and wizened and old, with yellow, flabby jaws, a neck like the throat of an alligator, and straight, white hair that stood from her head uncannily stiff.

" But the demoiselle wishes to appear a boy, un petit garçon?" she inquired, gazing eagerly at Flo's long, slender frame. Her voice was old and thin, like the high quavering of an imperfect tuning-fork, and her eyes were sharp as talons in their grasping glance.

" Mademoiselle does not wish such a costume," gruffly responded Mephisto.

" Ma foi, there is no other," said the ancient, shrugging her shoulders. "But one is left now; mademoiselle would make a fine troubadour."

"Flo," said Mephisto, "it's a dare-
devil scheme, try it; no one will ever
know it but us, and we'll die before
we tell. Besides, we must; it's late,
and you couldn't find your crowd."

And that was why you might have
seen a Mephisto and a slender troubadour of lovely form, with mandolin
flung across his shoulder, followed by
a bevy of jockeys and ballet girls,
laughing and singing as they swept
down Rampart Street.

When the flash and glare and bril-
liancy of Canal Street have palled upon
the tired eye, when it is yet too soon
to go home to such a prosaic thing as
dinner, and one still wishes for novelty,
then it is wise to go into the lower dis-
tricts. There is fantasy and fancy and
grotesqueness run wild in the costum-
ing and the behaviour of the maskers.
Such dances and whoops and leaps as
these hideous Indians and devils do in-

dulge in; such wild curvetings and long walks! In the open squares, where whole groups do congregate, it is wonderfully amusing. Then, too, there is a ball in every available hall, a delirious ball, where one may dance all day for ten cents; dance and grow mad for joy, and never know who were your companions, and be yourself unknown. And in the exhilaration of the day, one walks miles and miles, and dances and skips, and the fatigue is never felt.

In Washington Square, away down where Royal Street empties its stream of children great and small into the broad channel of Elysian Fields Avenue, there was a perfect Indian pow-wow. With a little imagination one might have willed away the vision of the surrounding houses, and fancied one's self again in the forest, where the natives were holding a sacred riot. The square was filled with spectators, masked and un-

masked.   It was amusing to watch
these mimic Red-men, they seemed so
fierce and earnest.

Suddenly one chief touched another
on the elbow.   " See that Mephisto
and troubadour over there ? " he whispered huskily.

" Yes ; who are they ? "

" I don't know the devil," responded
the other, quietly, " but I 'd know that
other form anywhere.   It 's Leon, see ?
I know those white hands like a woman's
and that restless head.   Ha ! "

" But there may be a mistake."

" No.   I 'd know that one anywhere ;
I feel it is he.   I 'll pay him now.   Ah,
sweetheart, you 've waited long, but
you shall feast now ! "   He was caressing something long and lithe and glittering beneath his blanket.

In a masked dance it is easy to give
a death-blow between the shoulders.
Two crowds meet and laugh and shout

and mingle almost inextricably, and if a shriek of pain should arise, it is not noticed in the din, and when they part, if one should stagger and fall bleeding to the ground, can any one tell who has given the blow? There is nothing but an unknown stiletto on the ground, the crowd has dispersed, and masks tell no tales anyway. There is murder, but by whom? for what? *Quien sabe?*

And that is how it happened on Carnival night, in the last mad moments of Rex's reign, a broken-hearted mother sat gazing wide-eyed and mute at a horrible something that lay across the bed. Outside the long sweet march music of many bands floated in as if in mockery, and the flash of rockets and Bengal lights illumined the dead, white face of the girl troubadour.

LITTLE MISS SOPHIE

LITTLE MISS SOPHIE

WHEN Miss Sophie knew consciousness again, the long, faint, swelling
notes of the organ were dying away in
distant echoes through the great arches
of the silent church, and she was alone,
crouching in a little, forsaken black
heap at the altar of the Virgin. The
twinkling tapers shone pityingly upon
her, the beneficent smile of the white-
robed Madonna seemed to whisper
comfort. A long gust of chill air swept
up the aisles, and Miss Sophie shivered
not from cold, but from nervousness.

But darkness was falling, and soon
the lights would be lowered, and the
great massive doors would be closed; so,
gathering her thin little cape about her
frail shoulders, Miss Sophie hurried

out, and along the brilliant noisy streets
home.

It was a wretched, lonely little room,
where the cracks let the boisterous
wind whistle through, and the smoky,
grimy walls looked cheerless and un-
homelike. A miserable little room in a
miserable little cottage in one of the
squalid streets of the Third District
that nature and the city fathers seemed
to have forgotten.

As bare and comfortless as the
room was Miss Sophie's life. She
rented these four walls from an un-
kempt little Creole woman, whose
progeny seemed like the promised
offspring of Abraham. She scarcely
kept the flickering life in her pale
little body by the unceasing toil of a
pair of bony hands, stitching, stitching,
ceaselessly, wearingly, on the bands and
pockets of trousers. It was her bread,
this monotonous, unending work; and

though whole days and nights constant labour brought but the most meagre recompense, it was her only hope of life.

She sat before the little charcoal brazier and warmed her transparent, needle-pricked fingers, thinking meanwhile of the strange events of the day. She had been up town to carry the great, black bundle of coarse pants and vests to the factory and to receive her small pittance, and on the way home stopped in at the Jesuit Church to say her little prayer at the altar of the calm white Virgin. There had been a wondrous burst of music from the great organ as she knelt there, an overpowering perfume of many flowers, the glittering dazzle of many lights, and the dainty frou-frou made by the silken skirts of wedding guests. So Miss Sophie stayed to the wedding; for what feminine heart, be it ever so old and seared, does not delight in one? And why should not a poor little Creole old maid be interested too?

Then the wedding party had filed in solemnly, to the rolling, swelling tones of the organ. Important-looking groomsmen; dainty, fluffy, white-robed maids; stately, satin-robed, illusion-veiled bride, and happy groom. She leaned forward to catch a better glimpse of their faces. "Ah!"—

Those near the Virgin's altar who heard a faint sigh and rustle on the steps glanced curiously as they saw a slight black-robed figure clutch the railing and lean her head against it. Miss Sophie had fainted.

"I must have been hungry," she mused over the charcoal fire in her little room, "I must have been hungry;" and she smiled a wan smile, and busied herself getting her evening meal of coffee and bread and ham.

If one were given to pity, the first

thought that would rush to one's lips
at sight of Miss Sophie would have
been, "Poor little woman!"   She had
come among the bareness and sordid-
ness of this neighbourhood five years
ago, robed in crape, and crying with
great sobs that seemed to shake the
vitality out of her.   Perfectly silent, too,
she was about her former life; but for
all that, Michel, the quartee grocer at
the corner, and Madame Laurent, who
kept the rabbé shop opposite, had fixed it
all up between them, of her sad history
and past glories.   Not that they knew;
but then Michel must invent something
when the neighbours came to him as
their fountain-head of wisdom.

One morning little Miss Sophie
opened wide her dingy windows to
catch the early freshness of the autumn
wind as it whistled through the yellow-
leafed trees.   It was one of those calm,
blue-misted, balmy, November days

that New Orleans can have when all
the rest of the country is fur-wrapped.
Miss Sophie pulled her machine to the
window, where the sweet, damp wind
could whisk among her black locks.

Whirr, whirr, went the machine, tick-
ing fast and lightly over the belts of
the rough jeans pants. Whirr, whirr,
yes, and Miss Sophie was actually
humming a tune! She felt strangely
light to-day.

"Ma foi," muttered Michel, strolling
across the street to where Madame
Laurent sat sewing behind the counter
on blue and brown-checked aprons,
"but the little ma'amselle sings. Perhaps she recollects."

"Perhaps," muttered the rabbé
woman.

But little Miss Sophie felt restless.
A strange impulse seemed drawing her
up town, and the machine seemed to
run slow, slow, before it would stitch

all of the endless number of jeans belts.
Her fingers trembled with nervous haste
as she pinned up the unwieldy black
bundle of finished work, and her feet
fairly tripped over each other in their
eagerness to get to Claiborne Street,
where she could board the up-town car.
There was a feverish desire to go some-
where, a sense of elation, a foolish
happiness that brought a faint echo of
colour into her pinched cheeks. She
wondered why.

No one noticed her in the car. Passengers on the Claiborne line are too
much accustomed to frail little black-
robed women with big, black bundles;
it is one of the city's most pitiful sights.
She leaned her head out of the window to catch a glimpse of the oleanders
on Bayou Road, when her attention
was caught by a conversation in the
car.

"Yes, it's too bad for Neale, and

lately married too," said the elder man. "I can't see what he is to do."

Neale! She pricked up her ears. That was the name of the groom in the Jesuit Church.

"How did it happen?" languidly inquired the younger. He was a stranger, evidently; a stranger with a high regard for the faultlessness of male attire.

"Well, the firm failed first; he did n't mind that much, he was so sure of his uncle's inheritance repairing his lost fortunes; but suddenly this difficulty of identification springs up, and he is literally on the verge of ruin."

"Won't some of you fellows who 've known him all your lives do to identify him?"

"Gracious man, we 've tried; but the absurd old will expressly stipulates that he shall be known only by a certain quaint Roman ring, and unless he has it, no identification, no fortune. He has given the ring away, and that settles it."

"Well, you're all chumps. Why doesn't he get the ring from the owner?"

"Easily said; but — it seems that Neale had some little Creole love-affair some years ago, and gave this ring to his dusky-eyed fiancée. You know how Neale is with his love-affairs, went off and forgot the girl in a month. It seems, however, she took it to heart, — so much so that he's ashamed to try to find her or the ring."

Miss Sophie heard no more as she gazed out into the dusty grass. There were tears in her eyes, hot blinding ones that wouldn't drop for pride, but stayed and scalded. She knew the story, with all its embellishment of heartaches. She knew the ring, too. She remembered the day she had kissed and wept and fondled it, until it seemed

10

her heart must burst under its load of grief before she took it to the pawn-broker's that another might be eased before the end came, — that other her father. The little " Creole love affair" of Neale's had not always been poor and old and jaded-looking; but reverses must come, even Neale knew that, so the ring was at the Mont de Piété. Still he must have it, it was his; it would save him from disgrace and suf-fering and from bringing the white-gowned bride into sorrow. He must have it; but how?

There it was still at the pawn-broker's; no one would have such an odd jewel, and the ticket was home in the bureau drawer. Well, he must have it; she might starve in the attempt. Such a thing as going to him and telling him that he might redeem it was an impos-sibility. That good, straight-backed, stiff-necked Creole blood would have

risen in all its strength and choked her.
No; as a present had the quaint Roman
circlet been placed upon her finger, as
a present should it be returned.

The bumping car rode slowly, and
the hot thoughts beat heavily in her
poor little head.   He must have the
ring; but how—the ring—the Roman
ring — the white-robed bride starving
— she was going mad — ah yes — the
church.

There it was, right in the busiest,
most bustling part of the town, its
fresco and bronze and iron quaintly
suggestive of mediæval times.   Within,
all was cool and dim and restful, with
the faintest whiff of lingering incense
rising and pervading the gray arches.
Yes, the Virgin would know and have
pity ; the sweet, white-robed Virgin at
the pretty flower-decked altar, or the
one away up in the niche, far above the
golden dome where the Host was.

Titiche, the busybody of the house, noticed that Miss Sophie's bundle was larger than usual that afternoon. "Ah, poor woman!" sighed Titiche's mother, "she would be rich for Christmas."

The bundle grew larger each day, and Miss Sophie grew smaller. The damp, cold rain and mist closed the white-curtained window, but always there behind the sewing-machine drooped and bobbed the little black-robed figure. Whirr, whirr went the wheels, and the coarse jeans pants piled in great heaps at her side. The Claiborne Street car saw her oftener than before, and the sweet white Virgin in the flowered niche above the gold-domed altar smiled at the little supplicant almost every day.

"Ma foi," said the slatternly land-lady to Madame Laurent and Michel one day, "I no see how she live! Eat? Nothin', nothin', almos', and las' night when it was so cold and foggy, eh? I hav' to mek him build fire. She mos' freeze."

Whereupon the rumour spread that Miss Sophie was starving herself to death to get some luckless relative out of jail for Christmas; a rumour which enveloped her scraggy little figure with a kind of halo to the neighbours when she appeared on the streets.

November had merged into December, and the little pile of coins was yet far from the sum needed. Dear God! how the money did have to go! The rent and the groceries and the coal, though, to be sure, she used a precious bit of that. Would all the work and saving and skimping do good? Maybe, yes, maybe by Christmas.

Christmas Eve on Royal Street is no place for a weakling, for the shouts and carousals of the roisterers will strike fear into the bravest ones. Yet amid the cries and yells, the deafening blow of horns and tin whistles, and the really dangerous fusillade of fireworks, a little figure hurried along, one hand clutching tightly the battered hat that the rude merry-makers had torn off, the other grasping under the thin black cape a worn little pocketbook.

Into the Mont de Piété she ran breathless, eager. The ticket? Here, worn, crumpled. The ring? It was not gone? No, thank Heaven! It was a joy well worth her toil, she thought, to have it again.

Had Titiche not been shooting crackers on the banquette instead of peering into the crack, as was his wont, his big, round black eyes would have grown saucer-wide to see little Miss Sophie kiss and fondle a ring, an ugly clumsy band of gold.

"Ah, dear ring," she murmured, "once you were his, and you shall be his again. You shall be on his finger,

and perhaps touch his heart. Dear ring,
ma chère petite de ma cœur, chérie
de ma cœur. Je t'aime, je t'aime, oui,
oui. You are his; you were mine once
too. To-night, just one night, I'll
keep you — then — to-morrow, you
shall go where you can save him."

The loud whistles and horns of the
little ones rose on the balmy air next
morning. No one would doubt it was
Christmas Day, even if doors and windows were open wide to let in cool air.
Why, there was Christmas even in the
very look of the mules on the poky
cars; there was Christmas noise in the
streets, and Christmas toys and Christmas odours, savoury ones that made the
nose wrinkle approvingly, issuing from
the kitchen. Michel and Madame
Laurent smiled greetings across the
street at each other, and the salutation
from a passer-by recalled the many-
progenied landlady to herself.

"Miss Sophie, well, po' soul, not ver' much Chris'mas for her. Mais, I'll jus' call him in fo' to spen' the day with me. Eet'll cheer her a bit."

It was so clean and orderly within the poor little room. Not a speck of dust or a litter of any kind on the quaint little old-time high bureau, unless you might except a sheet of paper lying loose with something written on it. Titiche had evidently inherited his prying propensities, for the landlady turned it over and read, —

Louis, — Here is the ring. I return it to you. I heard you needed it. I hope it comes not too late.   Sophie.

"The ring, where?" muttered the landlady. There it was, clasped between her fingers on her bosom, — a bosom white and cold, under a cold happy face. Christmas had indeed dawned for Miss Sophie.

SISTER JOSEPHA

SISTER JOSEPHA

SISTER JOSEPHA told her beads me-
chanically, her fingers numb with the
accustomed exercise. The little organ
creaked a dismal "O Salutaris," and
she still knelt on the floor, her white-
bonneted head nodding suspiciously.
The Mother Superior gave a sharp
glance at the tired figure; then, as a
sudden lurch forward brought the little
sister back to consciousness, Mother's
eyes relaxed into a genuine smile.

The bell tolled the end of vespers, and
the sombre-robed nuns filed out of the
chapel to go about their evening duties.
Little Sister Josepha's work was to
attend to the household lamps, but
there must have been as much oil
spilled upon the table to-night as was

put in the vessels. The small brown hands trembled so that most of the wicks were trimmed with points at one corner which caused them to smoke that night.

"Oh, cher Seigneur," she sighed, giving an impatient polish to a refractory chimney, "it is wicked and sinful, I know, but I am so tired. I can't be happy and sing any more. It does n't seem right for le bon Dieu to have me all cooped up here with nothing to see but stray visitors, and always the same old work, teaching those mean little girls to sew, and washing and filling the same old lamps. Pah!" And she polished the chimney with a sudden vigorous jerk which threatened destruction.

They were rebellious prayers that the red mouth murmured that night, and a restless figure that tossed on the hard dormitory bed. Sister Dominica

called from her couch to know if Sister
Josepha were ill.

"No," was the somewhat short response; then a muttered, "Why can't
they let me alone for a minute? That
pale-eyed Sister Dominica never sleeps;
that's why she is so ugly."

About fifteen years before this night
some one had brought to the orphan
asylum connected with this convent, du
Sacré Cœur, a round, dimpled bit of
three-year-old humanity, who regarded
the world from a pair of gravely twinkling black eyes, and only took a chubby
thumb out of a rosy mouth long enough
to answer in monosyllabic French. It
was a child without an identity; there
was but one name that any one seemed
to know, and that, too, was vague,—
Camille.

She grew up with the rest of the
waifs; scraps of French and American
civilization thrown together to develop

a seemingly inconsistent miniature world. Mademoiselle Camille was a queen among them, a pretty little tyrant who ruled the children and dominated the more timid sisters in charge.

One day an awakening came. When she was fifteen, and almost fully ripened into a glorious tropical beauty of the type that matures early, some visitors to the convent were fascinated by her and asked the Mother Superior to give the girl into their keeping.

Camille fled like a frightened fawn into the yard, and was only unearthed with some difficulty from behind a group of palms. Sulky and pouting, she was led into the parlour, picking at her blue pinafore like a spoiled infant.

"The lady and gentleman wish you to go home with them, Camille," said the Mother Superior, in the language of the convent. Her voice was kind and gentle apparently; but the child, accus-

tomed to its various inflections, detected
a steely ring behind its sòftness, like the
proverbial iron hand in the velvet glove.

"You must understand, madame,"
continued Mother, in stilted English,
"that we never force children from us.
We are ever glad to place them in comfortable — how you say that? — quar-
ters — maisons — homes — bien! But
we will not make them go if they do
not wish."

Camille stole a glance at her would-
be guardians, and decided instantly, im-
pulsively, finally. The woman suited
her; but the man! It was doubtless
intuition of the quick, vivacious sort
which belonged to her blood that served
her. Untutored in worldly knowledge,
she could not divine the meaning of the
pronounced leers and admiration of her
physical charms which gleamed in the
man's face, but she knew it made her
feel creepy, and stoutly refused to go.

Next day Camille was summoned from a task to the Mother Superior's parlour. The other girls gazed with envy upon her as she dashed down the courtyard with impetuous movement. Camille, they decided crossly, received too much notice. It was Camille this, Camille that; she was pretty, it was to be expected. Even Father Ray lingered longer in his blessing when his hands pressed her silky black hair.

As she entered the parlour, a strange chill swept over the girl. The room was not an unaccustomed one, for she had swept it many times, but to-day the stiff black chairs, the dismal crucifixes, the gleaming whiteness of the walls, even the cheap lithograph of the Madonna which Camille had always regarded as a perfect specimen of art, seemed cold and mean.

"Camille, ma chère," said Mother, "I am extremely displeased with you.

Why did you not wish to go with
Monsieur and Madame Lafayé yesterday?"

The girl uncrossed her hands from
her bosom, and spread them out in a
deprecating gesture.

"Mais, ma mère, I was afraid."

Mother's face grew stern. "No foolishness now," she exclaimed.

"It is not foolishness, ma mère; I
could not help it, but that man looked
at me so funny, I felt all cold chills
down my back. Oh, dear Mother, I
love the convent and the sisters so, I
just want to stay and be a sister too,
may I?"

And thus it was that Camille took
the white veil at sixteen years. Now
that the period of novitiate was over, it
was just beginning to dawn upon her
that she had made a mistake.

"Maybe it would have been better
had I gone with the funny-looking lady

11

and gentleman," she mused bitterly one night. "Oh, Seigneur, I'm so tired and impatient; it's so dull here, and, dear God, I'm so young."

There was no help for it. One must arise in the morning, and help in the refectory with the stupid Sister Francesca, and go about one's duties with a prayerful mien, and not even let a sigh escape when one's head ached with the eternal telling of beads.

A great fête day was coming, and an atmosphere of preparation and mild excitement pervaded the brown walls of the convent like a delicate aroma. The old Cathedral around the corner had stood a hundred years, and all the city was rising to do honour to its age and time-softened beauty. There would be a service, oh, but such a one! with two Cardinals, and Archbishops and Bishops, and all the accompanying glitter of soldiers and orchestras. The

little sisters of the Convent du Sacré
Cœur clasped their hands in anticipation of the holy joy. Sister Josepha
curled her lip, she was so tired of
churchly pleasures.

The day came, a gold and blue spring
day, when the air hung heavy with
the scent of roses and magnolias, and
the sunbeams fairly laughed as they
kissed the houses. The old Cathedral
stood gray and solemn, and the flowers
in Jackson Square smiled cheery birthday greetings across the way. The
crowd around the door surged and
pressed and pushed in its eagerness to
get within. Ribbons stretched across
the banquette were of no avail to re-
press it, and important ushers with
cardinal colours could do little more.

The Sacred Heart sisters filed slowly
in at the side door, creating a momentary flutter as they paced reverently to
their seats, guarding the blue-bonneted

orphans. Sister Josepha, determined to see as much of the world as she could, kept her big black eyes opened wide, as the church rapidly filled with the fashionably dressed, perfumed, rustling, and self-conscious throng.

Her heart beat quickly. The rebellious thoughts that will arise in the most philosophical of us surged in her small heavily gowned bosom. For her were the gray things, the neutral tinted skies, the ugly garb, the coarse meats; for them the rainbow, the ethereal airiness of earthly joys, the bonbons and glacés of the world. Sister Josepha did not know that the rainbow is elusive, and its colours but the illumination of tears ; she had never been told that earthly ethereality is necessarily ephemeral, nor that bonbons and glacés, whether of the palate or of the soul, nauseate and pall upon the taste. Dear God, forgive her, for she bent with

contrite tears over her worn rosary, and
glanced no more at the worldly glitter
of femininity.

The sunbeams streamed through the
high windows in purple and crimson
lights upon a veritable fugue of colour.
Within the seats, crush upon crush of
spring millinery ; within the aisles erect
lines of gold-braided, gold-buttoned
military. Upon the altar, broad sweeps
of golden robes, great dashes of crimson
skirts, mitres and gleaming crosses, the
soft neutral hue of rich lace vestments ;
the tender heads of childhood in picturesque attire; the proud, golden mag-
nificence of the domed altar with
its weighting mass of lilies and wide-
eyed roses, and the long candles that
sparkled their yellow star points above
the reverent throng within the altar
rails.

The soft baritone of the Cardinal
intoned a single phrase in the suspended

silence. The censer took up the note in
its delicate clink clink, as it swung to and
fro in the hands of a fair-haired child.
Then the organ, pausing an instant in
a deep, mellow, long-drawn note, burst
suddenly into a magnificent strain, and
the choir sang forth, "Kyrie Eleïson,
Christe Eleïson." One voice, flute-like,
piercing, sweet, rang high over the rest.
Sister Josepha heard and trembled, as
she buried her face in her hands, and let
her tears fall, like other beads, through
her rosary.

It was when the final word of the
service had been intoned, the last peal
of the exit march had died away, that
she looked up meekly, to encounter a
pair of youthful brown eyes gazing
pityingly upon her. That was all she
remembered for a moment, that the
eyes were youthful and handsome and
tender. Later, she saw that they were
placed in a rather beautiful boyish face,

surmounted by waves of brown hair,
curling and soft, and that the head was
set on a pair of shoulders decked in
military uniform.   Then the brown
eyes marched away with the rest of the
rear guard, and the white-bonneted sisters filed out the side door, through
the narrow court, back into the brown
convent.

That night Sister Josepha tossed
more than usual on her hard bed,
and clasped her fingers often in prayer
to quell the wickedness in her heart.
Turn where she would, pray as she
might, there was ever a pair of tender,
pitying brown eyes, haunting her persis-
tently.   The squeaky organ at vespers
intoned the clank of military accoutre-
ments to her ears, the white bonnets of
the sisters about her faded into mists
of curling brown hair.   Briefly, Sister
Josepha was in love.

The days went on pretty much as

before, save for the one little heart that beat rebelliously now and then, though it tried so hard to be submissive. There was the morning work in the refectory, the stupid little girls to teach sewing, and the insatiable lamps that were so greedy for oil. And always the tender, boyish brown eyes, that looked so sorrowfully at the fragile, beautiful little sister, haunting, following, pleading.

Perchance, had Sister Josepha been in the world, the eyes would have been an incident. But in this home of self-repression and retrospection, it was a life-story. The eyes had gone their way, doubtless forgetting the little sister they pitied; but the little sister?

The days glided into weeks, the weeks into months. Thoughts of escape had come to Sister Josepha, to flee into the world, to merge in the great city where recognition was impossible, and, working her way like the rest

of humanity, perchance encounter the
eyes again.

It was all planned and ready. She
would wait until some morning when
the little band of black-robed sisters
wended their way to mass at the Cathedral. When it was time to file out the
side-door into the courtway, she would
linger at prayers, then slip out another
door, and unseen glide up Chartres
Street to Canal, and once there, mingle
in the throng that filled the wide
thoroughfare. Beyond this first plan
she could think no further. Penniless,
garbed, and shaven though she would
be, other difficulties never presented
themselves to her. She would rely on
the mercies of the world to help her
escape from this torturing life of inertia.
It seemed easy now that the first step
of decision had been taken.

The Saturday night before the final
day had come, and she lay feverishly

nervous in her narrow little bed, won-
dering with wide-eyed fear at the morrow. Pale-eyed Sister Dominica and
Sister Francesca were whispering together in the dark silence, and Sister
Josepha's ears pricked up as she heard
her name.

"She is not well, poor child," said
Francesca. "I fear the life is too
confining."

"It is best for her," was the reply.
"You know, sister, how hard it would
be for her in the world, with no name
but Camille, no friends, and her beauty;
and then —"

Sister Josepha heard no more, for
her heart beating tumultously in her
bosom drowned the rest. Like the rush
of the bitter salt tide over a drowning
man clinging to a spar, came the com-
plete submerging of her hopes of
another life. No name but Camille,
that was true; no nationality, for she

could never tell from whom or whence
she came; no friends, and a beauty
that not even an ungainly bonnet and
shaven head could hide. In a flash she
realised the deception of the life she
would lead, and the cruel self-torture
of wonder at her own identity. Already,
as if in anticipation of the world's ques-
tionings, she was asking herself, " Who
am I ? What am I ? "

The next morning the sisters du
Sacré Cœur filed into the Cathedral at
High Mass, and bent devout knees
at the general confession. " Confiteor
Deo omnipotenti," murmured the priest;
and tremblingly one little sister followed
the words, " Je confesse à Dieu, tout
puissant — que j'ai beaucoup péché par
pensées — c'est ma faute — c'est ma
faute — c'est ma très grande faute."

The organ pealed forth as mass
ended, the throng slowly filed out, and
the sisters paced through the courtway

back into the brown convent walls. One paused at the entrance, and gazed with swift longing eyes in the direction of narrow, squalid Chartres Street, then, with a gulping sob, followed the rest, and vanished behind the heavy door.

THE PRALINE WOMAN

THE PRALINE WOMAN

THE praline woman sits by the side of the Archbishop's quaint little old chapel on Royal Street, and slowly waves her latanier fan over the pink and brown wares.

" Pralines, pralines. Ah, ma'amzelle, you buy? S'il vous plaît, ma'amzelle, ces pralines, dey be fine, ver' fresh.

" Mais non, maman, you are not sure?

" Sho', chile, ma bébé, ma petite, she put dese up hissef. He's hans' so small, ma'amzelle, lak you's, mais brune. She put dese up dis morn'. You tak' none? No husban' fo' you den!

" Ah, ma petite, you tak'? Cinq sous, bébé, may le bon Dieu keep you good !

"Mais oui, madame, I know you étrangér. You don' look lak dese New Orleans peop'. You lak' dose Yankee dat come down 'fo' de war."

Ding-dong, ding-dong, ding-dong, chimes the Cathedral bell across Jackson Square, and the praline woman crosses herself.

"Hail, Mary, full of grace —

"Pralines, madame? You buy lak' dat? Dix sous, madame, an' one lil' piece fo' lagniappe fo' madame's lil' bébé. Ah, c'est bon!

"Pralines, pralines, so fresh, so fine! M'sieu would lak' some fo' he's lil' gal' at home? Mais non, what's dat you say? She's daid! Ah, m'sieu, 't is my lil' gal what died long year ago. Misère, misère!

"Here come dat lazy Indien squaw. What she good fo', anyhow? She jes' sit lak dat in de French Market an' sell her filé, an' sleep, sleep, sleep, lak'

so in he's blanket. Hey, dere, you,
Tonita, how goes you' beezness?

"Pralines, pralines! Holy Father,
you give me dat blessin' sho'? Tak'
one, I know you lak dat w'ite one. It
tas' good, I know, bien.

"Pralines, madame? I lak' you'
face. What fo' you wear black? You'
lil' boy daid? You tak' one, jes' see
how it tas'. I had one lil' boy once,
he jes' grow 'twell he's big lak' dis,
den one day he tak' sick an' die. Oh,
madame, it mos' brek my po' heart. I
burn candle in St. Rocque, I say my
beads, I sprinkle holy water roun' he's
bed; he jes' lay so, he's eyes turn up,
he say 'Maman, maman,' den he die!
Madame, you tak' one. Non, non, no
l'argent, you tak' one fo' my lil' boy's
sake.

"Pralines, pralines, m'sieu? Who
mak' dese? My lil' gal, Didele, of
co'se. Non, non, I don't mak' no mo'.

Po' Tante Marie get too ol'.   Didele?
She's one lil' gal I 'dopt.   I see her one
day in de strit.   He walk so; hit col'
she shiver, an' I say, 'Where you gone,
lil' gal?' and he can' tell.   He jes' crip
close to me, an' cry so!   Den I tak'
her home wid me, and she say he's
name Didele.   You see dey wa'nt no-
body dere.   My lil' gal, she's daid of de
yellow fever; my lil' boy, he's daid, po'
Tante Marie all alone.   Didele, she
grow fine, she keep house an' mek'
pralines.   Den, when night come, she
sit wid he's guitar an' sing,

> " ' Tu l'aime ces trois jours,
> Tu l'aime ces trois jours,
> Ma cœur à toi,
> Ma cœur à toi,
> Tu l'aime ces trois jours ! '

"Ah, he's fine gal, is Didele!

"Pralines, pralines!   Dat lil' cloud,
h'it look lak' rain, I hope no.

"Here come dat lazy I'ishman down

de strit.   I don't lak' I'ishman, me,
non, dey so funny.   One day one
I'ishman, he say to me, 'Auntie, what
fo' you talk so?' and I jes' say back,
'What fo' you say "Faith an' be
jabers"?'   Non, I don' lak I'ishman,
me!

"Here come de rain!   Now I got
fo' to go.   Didele, she be wait fo' me.
Down h'it come!   H'it fall in de
Meesseesip, an' fill up — up — so,
clean to de levee, den we have big cri-
vasse, an' po' Tante Marie float away.
Bon jour, madame, you come again?
Pralines!   Pralines!"

ODALIE

ODALIE

Now and then Carnival time comes at the time of the good Saint Valentine, and then sometimes it comes as late as the warm days in March, when spring is indeed upon us, and the greenness of the grass outvies the green in the royal standards.

Days and days before the Carnival proper, New Orleans begins to take on a festive appearance. Here and there the royal flags with their glowing greens and violets and yellows appear, and then, as if by magic, the streets and buildings flame and burst like poppies out of bud, into a glorious refulgence of colour that steeps the senses into a languorous acceptance of warmth and beauty.

On Mardi Gras day, as you know, it is a town gone mad with folly. A huge masked ball emptied into the streets at daylight; a meeting of all nations on common ground, a pot-pourri of every conceivable human ingredient, but faintly describes it all. There are music and flowers, cries and laughter and song and joyousness, and never an aching heart to show its sorrow or dim the happiness of the streets. A wondrous thing, this Carnival!

But the old cronies down in French-town, who know everything, and can recite you many a story, tell of one sad heart on Mardi Gras years ago. It was a woman's, of course; for "Il est toujours les femmes qui sont malheureuses," says an old proverb, and perhaps it is right. This woman — a child, she would be called elsewhere, save in this land of tropical growth and pre-cocity — lost her heart to one who

never knew, a very common story, by
the way, but one which would have
been quite distasteful to the haughty
judge, her father, had he known.

Odalie was beautiful. Odalie was
haughty too, but gracious enough to
those who pleased her dainty fancy.
In the old French house on Royal
Street, with its quaint windows and
Spanish courtyard green and cool,
and made musical by the plashing of
the fountain and the trill of caged birds,
lived Odalie in convent-like seclusion.
Monsieur le Juge was determined no
hawk should break through the cage
and steal his dove ; and so, though there
was no mother, a stern duenna aunt
kept faithful watch.

Alas for the precautions of la Tante !
Bright eyes that search for other bright
eyes in which lurks the spirit of youth
and mischief are ever on the look-out,
even in church. Dutifully was Odalie

marched to the Cathedral every Sunday
to mass, and Tante Louise, nodding devoutly over her beads, could not see
the blushes and glances full of meaning,
a whole code of signals as it were, that
passed between Odalie and Pierre, the
impecunious young clerk in the court-
room.

Odalie loved, perhaps, because there
was not much else to do. When one
is shut up in a great French house with
a grim sleepy tante and no companions
of one's own age, life becomes a dull
thing, and one is ready for any new
sensation, particularly if in the veins
there bounds the tempestuous Spanish-
French blood that Monsieur le Juge
boasted of. So Odalie hugged the
image of her Pierre during the week
days, and played tremulous little love-
songs to it in the twilight when la Tante
dozed over her devotion book, and on
Sundays at mass there were glances

and blushes, and mayhap, at some especially remembered time, the touch of finger-tips at the holy-water font, while la Tante dropped her last genuflexion.

Then came the Carnival time, and one little heart beat faster, as the gray house on Royal Street hung out its many-hued flags, and draped its grim front with glowing colours. It was to be a time of joy and relaxation, when every one could go abroad, and in the crowds one could speak to whom one chose. Unconscious plans formulated, and the petite Odalie was quite happy as the time drew near.

"Only think, Tante Louise," she would cry, "what a happy time it is to be!"

But Tante Louise only grumbled, as was her wont.

It was Mardi Gras day at last, and early through her window Odalie could hear the jingle of folly bells on the maskers' costumes, the tinkle of music, and the echoing strains of songs. Up to her ears there floated the laughter of the older maskers, and the screams of the little children frightened at their own images under the mask and domino. What a hurry to be out and in the motley merry throng, to be pacing Royal Street to Canal Street, where was life and the world !

They were tired eyes with which Odalie looked at the gay pageant at last, tired with watching throng after throng of maskers, of the unmasked, of peering into the cartsful of singing minstrels, into carriages of revellers, hoping for a glimpse of Pierre the devout. The allegorical carts rumbling by with their important red-clothed horses were beginning to lose charm, the disguises showed tawdry, even the gay-hued flags fluttered sadly to Odalie.

Mardi Gras was a tiresome day, after
all, she sighed, and Tante Louise agreed
with her for once.

Six o'clock had come, the hour when
all masks must be removed. The long
red rays of the setting sun glinted
athwart the many-hued costumes of
the revellers trooping unmasked home-
ward to rest for the night's last mad
frolic.

Down Toulouse Street there came
the merriest throng of all. Young
men and women in dainty, fairy-like
garb, dancers, and dresses of the picturesque Empire, a butterfly or two and
a dame here and there with powdered
hair and graces of olden time. Singing with unmasked faces, they danced
toward Tante Louise and Odalie. She
stood with eyes lustrous and tear-heavy,
for there in the front was Pierre, Pierre
the faithless, his arms about the slender waist of a butterfly, whose tinselled

powdered hair floated across the lace
ruffles of his Empire coat.

" Pierre ! " cried Odalie, softly.   No
one heard, for it was a mere faint breath
and fell unheeded.   Instead the laughing throng pelted her with flowers and
candy and went their way, and even
Pierre did not see.

You see, when one is shut up in the
grim walls of a Royal Street house, with
no one but a Tante Louise and a grim
judge, how is one to learn that in this
world there are faithless ones who may
glance tenderly into one's eyes at mass
and pass the holy water on caressing
fingers without being madly in love?
There was no one to tell Odalie, so she
sat at home in the dull first days of
Lent, and nursed her dear dead love,
and mourned as women have done from
time immemorial over the faithlessness
of man.   And when one day she asked
that she might go back to the Ursulines'

convent where her childish days were
spent, only to go this time as a nun,
Monsieur le Juge and Tante Louise
thought it quite the proper and con-
venient thing to do; for how were
they to know the secret of that Mardi
Gras day?

LA JUANITA

LA JUANITA

IF you never lived in Mandeville, you cannot appreciate the thrill of wholesome, satisfied joy which sweeps over its inhabitants every evening at five o'clock. It is the hour for the arrival of the " New Camelia," the happening of the day. As early as four o'clock the trailing smoke across the horizon of the treacherous Lake Pontchartrain appears, and Mandeville knows then that the hour for its siesta has passed, and that it must array itself in its coolest and fluffiest garments, and go down to the pier to meet this sole connection between itself and the outside world; the little, puffy, side-wheel steamer that comes daily from New Orleans and brings the mail and the news.

On this particular day there was an air of suppressed excitement about the little knot of people which gathered on the pier. To be sure, there were no outward signs to show that anything unusual had occurred. The small folks danced with the same glee over the worn boards, and peered down with daring excitement into the perilous depths of the water below. The sun, fast sinking in a gorgeous glow behind the pines of the Tchefuncta region far away, danced his mischievous rays in much the same manner that he did every other day. But there was a something in the air, a something not tangible, but mysterious, subtle. You could catch an indescribable whiff of it in your inner senses, by the half-eager, furtive glances that the small crowd cast at La Juanita.

"Gar, gar, le bateau!" said one dark-tressed mother to the wide-eyed baby. "Et, oui," she added, in an

undertone to her companion.   "Voilà,
La Juanita!"

La Juanita, you must know, was the
pride of Mandeville, the adored, the
admired of all, with her petite, half-
Spanish, half-French beauty.   Whether
rocking in the shade of the Cherokee-
rose-covered   gallery   of   Grandpère
Colomés' big house, her fair face bon-
net-shaded, her dainty hands gloved to
keep the sun from too close an ac-
quaintance, or splashing the spray from
the bow of her little pirogue, or fluffing
her skirts about her tiny feet on the
pier, she was the pet and ward of Mandeville, as it were, La Juanita Alvarez,
since Madame Alvarez was a widow,
and Grandpère Colomés was strict and
stern.

And now La Juanita had set her
small foot down with a passionate stamp
before Grandpère Colomés' very face,
and tossed her black curls about her

wilful head, and said she would go to
the pier this evening to meet her Mercer. All Mandeville knew this, and
cast its furtive glances alternately at La
Juanita with two big pink spots in her
cheeks, and at the entrance to the pier,
expecting Grandpère Colomés and a
scene.

The sun cast red glows and violet
shadows over the pier, and the pines
murmured a soft little vesper hymn
among themselves up on the beach, as
the " New Camelia " swung herself in,
crabby, sidewise, like a fat old gentleman going into a small door. There
was the clang of an important bell, the
scream of a hoarse little whistle, and
Mandeville rushed to the gang-plank
to welcome the outside world. Juanita
put her hand through a waiting arm,
and tripped away with her Mercer, big
and blond and brawny. " Un Américain, pah ! " said the little mother

of the black eyes. And Mandeville
sighed sadly, and shook its head, and
was sorry for Grandpère Colomés.

This was Saturday, and the big regatta would be Monday. Ah, that
regatta, such a one as Mandeville had
never seen! There were to be boats
from Madisonville and Amite, from
Lewisburg and Covington, and even
far-away Nott's Point. There was to
be a Class A and Class B and Class C,
and the little French girls of the town
flaunted their ribbons down the one
oak-shaded, lake-kissed street, and dared
anyone to say theirs were not the
favourite colours.

In Class A was entered, "' La Juanita,' captain Mercer Grangeman, colours pink and gold." Her name, her
colours; what impudence!

Of course, not being a Mandevillian,
you could not understand the shame
of Grandpère Colomés at this. Was it

not bad enough for his petite Juanita,
his Spanish blossom, his hope of a family that had held itself proudly aloof from
" dose Americain " from time immemorial, to have smiled upon this Mercer,
this pale-eyed youth ?   Was it not bad
enough for her to demean herself by
walking upon the pier with him ?   But
for a boat, his boat, "un bateau Américain," to be named La Juanita ! Oh,
the shame of it !   Grandpère Colomés
prayed a devout prayer to the Virgin
that " La Juanita " should be capsized.

Monday came, clear and blue and
stifling.   The waves of hot air danced
on the sands and adown the one street
merrily.   Glassily calm lay the Pontchartrain, heavily still hung the atmosphere.   Madame Alvarez cast an in-
quiring glance toward the sky.   Grandpère Colomés chuckled.   He had not
lived on the shores of the treacherous
Lake Pontchartrain for nothing.   He

knew its every mood, its petulances and passions; he knew this glassy warmth and what it meant. Chuckling again and again, he stepped to the gallery and looked out over the lake, and at the pier, where lay the boats rocking and idly tugging at their moorings. La Juanita in her rose-scented room tied the pink ribbons on her dainty frock, and fastened cloth of gold roses at her lithe waist.

It was said that just before the crack of the pistol La Juanita's tiny hand lay in Mercer's, and that he bent his head, and whispered softly, so that the surrounding crowd could not hear, —

"Juanita mine, if I win, you will?"

"Oui, mon Mercere, eef you win."

In another instant the white wings were off scudding before the rising breeze, dipping their glossy boat-sides into the clear water, straining their cordage in their tense efforts to reach

the stake boats. Mandeville indiscri-
minately distributed itself on piers, large
and small, bath-house tops, trees, and
craft of all kinds, from pirogue, dory,
and pine-raft to pretentious cat-boat
and shell-schooner. Mandeville cheered
and strained its eyes after all the boats,
but chiefly was its attention directed to
" La Juanita."

" Ah, voilà, eet is ahead ! "

" Mais non, c'est un autre ! "

" La Juanita !   La Juanita ! "

" Regardez Grandpère Colomés ! "

Old Colomés on the big pier with
Madame Alvarez and his granddaughter
was intently straining his weather-beaten
face in the direction of Nott's Point,
his back resolutely turned upon the
scudding white wings. A sudden
chuckle of grim satisfaction caused La
Petite's head to toss petulantly.

But only for a minute, for Grandpère
Colomés' chuckle was followed by a

shout of dismay from those whose glance had followed his. You must know that it is around Nott's Point that the storm king shows his wings first, for the little peninsula guards the entrance which leads into the southeast waters of the stormy Rigolets and the blustering Gulf. You would know, if you lived in Mandeville, that when the pines on Nott's Point darken and when the water shows white beyond like the teeth of a hungry wolf, it is time to steer your boat into the mouth of some one of the many calm bayous which flow silently throughout St. Tammany parish into the lake. Small wonder that the cry of dismay went up now, for Nott's Point was black, with a lurid light overhead, and the roar of the grim southeast wind came ominously over the water.

La Juanita clasped her hands and strained her eyes for her namesake.

The racers had rounded the second
stake-boat, and the course of the tri-
angle headed them directly for the lurid
cloud.

You should have seen Grandpère
Colomés then.   He danced up and
down the pier in a perfect frenzy. The
thin pale lips of Madame Alvarez
moved in a silent prayer; La Juanita
stood coldly silent.

And now you could see that the
advance guard of the southeast force
had struck the little fleet. They dipped
and scurried and rocked, and you could
see the sails being reefed hurriedly, and
almost hear the rigging creak and moan
under the strain.   Then the wind came
up the lake, and struck the town with a
tumultuous force. The waters rose and
heaved in the long, sullen ground-swell,
which betokened serious trouble. There
was a rush of lake-craft to shelter.
Heavy gray waves boomed against the

breakwaters and piers, dashing their
brackish spray upon the strained watch-
ers ; then with a shriek and a howl the
storm burst full, with blinding sheets of
rain, and a great hurricane of Gulf wind
that threatened to blow the little town
away.

La Juanita was proud. When Grandpère and Madame led her away in the
storm, though her face was white, and
the rose mouth pressed close, not a
word did she say, and her eyes were as
bright as ever before. It was foolish
to hope that the frail boats could sur-
vive such a storm. There was not even
the merest excuse for shelter out in the
waters, and when Lake Pontchartrain
grows angry, it devours without pity.

Your tropical storm is soon over,
however, and in an hour the sun strug-
gled through a gray and misty sky,
over which the wind was sweeping
great clouds. The rain-drops hung

diamond-like on the thick foliage, but the long ground-swell still boomed against the breakwaters and showed white teeth, far to the south.

As chickens creep from under shelter after a rain, so the people of Mandeville crept out again on the piers, on the bath-houses, on the breakwater edge, and watched eagerly for the boats. Slowly upon the horizon appeared white sails, and the little craft swung into sight. One, two, three, four, five, six, seven, eight, nine, counted Mandeville. Every one coming in! Bravo! And a great cheer that swept the whole length of the town from the post-office to Black Bayou went up. Bravo! Every boat was coming in. But — was every man?

This was a sobering thought, and in the hush which followed it you could hear the Q. and C. train thundering over the great lake-bridge, miles away.

Well, they came into the pier at last,
" La Juanita " in the lead; and as Captain Mercer landed, he was surrounded
by a voluble, chattering, anxious throng
that loaded him with questions in patois,
in broken English, and in French. He
was no longer " un Américain" now, he
was a hero.

When the other eight boats came in,
and Mandeville saw that no one was
lost, there was another ringing bravo,
and more chattering of questions.

We heard the truth finally. When
the storm burst, Captain Mercer suddenly promoted himself to an admiral-
ship and assumed command of his little
fleet. He had led them through the
teeth of the gale to a small inlet on the
coast between Bayou Lacombe and
Nott's Point, and there they had waited
until the storm passed. Loud were the
praises of the other captains for Admiral
Mercer, profuse were the thanks of the

sisters and sweethearts, as he was carried triumphantly on the shoulders of the sailors adown the wharf to the Maison Colomés.

The crispness had gone from Juanita's pink frock, and the cloth of gold roses were wellnigh petalless, but the hand that she slipped into his was warm and soft, and the eyes that were upturned to Mercer's blue ones were shining with admiring tears. And even Grandpère Colomés, as he brewed on the Cherokee-rose-covered gallery, a fiery punch for the heroes, was heard to admit that " some time dose Americain can mos' be lak one Frenchman."

And we danced at the betrothal supper the next week.

TITEE

TITEE

It was cold that day. The great sharp north-wind swept out Elysian Fields Street in blasts that made men shiver, and bent everything in their track. The skies hung lowering and gloomy; the usually quiet street was more than deserted, it was dismal.

Titee leaned against one of the brown freight cars for protection against the shrill norther, and warmed his little chapped hands at a blaze of chips and dry grass. "Maybe it 'll snow," he muttered, casting a glance at the sky that would have done credit to a practised seaman. "Then won't I have fun! Ugh, but the wind blows!"

It was Saturday, or Titee would have been in school, the big yellow school on Marigny Street, where he went every day when its bell boomed nine o'clock, went with a run and a joyous whoop, ostensibly to imbibe knowledge, really to make his teacher's life a burden.

Idle, lazy, dirty, troublesome boy, she called him to herself, as day by day wore on, and Titee improved not, but let his whole class pass him on its way to a higher grade. A practical joke he relished infinitely more than a practical problem, and a good game at pin-sticking was far more entertaining than a language lesson. Moreover, he was always hungry, and would eat in school before the half-past ten recess, thereby losing much good playtime for his voracious appetite.

But there was nothing in natural history that Titee did not know. He could dissect a butterfly or a mosquito hawk, and describe their parts as accurately as

a spectacled student with a scalpel and
microscope could talk about a cadaver.
The entire Third District, with its
swamps and canals and commons and
railroad sections, and its wondrous,
crooked, tortuous streets, was an open
book to Titee. There was not a nook
or corner that he did not know or
could not tell of. There was not a bit
of gossip among the gamins, little Creole and Spanish fellows, with dark skins
and lovely eyes, like spaniels, that
Titee could not tell of. He knew just
exactly when it was time for crawfish to
be plentiful down in the Claiborne and
Marigny canals; just when a poor,
breadless fellow might get a job in the
big bone-yard and fertilising factory,
out on the railroad track ; and as for
the levee, with its ships and schooners
and sailors, how he could revel in them !
The wondrous ships, the pretty little
schooners, where the foreign-looking

sailors lay on long moonlight nights, singing to their guitars and telling great stories, — all these things and more could Titee tell of. He had been down to the Gulf, and out on its treacherous waters through the Eads jetties on a fishing-smack with some jolly brown sailors, and could interest the whole school-room in the talk-lessons, if he chose.

Titee shivered as the wind swept round the freight-cars. There is n't much warmth in a bit of a jersey coat.

"Wish 'twas summer," he murmured, casting another sailor's glance at the sky. "Don't believe I like snow; it's too wet and cold." And with a last parting caress at the little fire he had builded for a minute's warmth, he plunged his hands in his pockets, shut his teeth, and started manfully on his mission out the railroad track toward the swamps.

It was late when Titee came home,
to such a home as it was, and he had
but illy performed his errand; so his
mother beat him and sent him to bed
supperless. A sharp strap stings in
cold weather, and a long walk in the
teeth of a biting wind creates a keen
appetite. But if Titee cried himself
to sleep that night, he was up bright
and early next morning, had been to
mass, devoutly kneeling on the cold
floor, blowing his fingers to keep them
warm, and was home almost before the
rest of the family were awake.

There was evidently some great
matter of business on the young man's
mind, for he scarcely ate his breakfast,
and left the table soon, eagerly cram-
ming the remainder of his meal in his
pockets.

" Ma foi, but what now ? " mused
his mother, as she watched his little
form sturdily trudging the track in the

face of the wind; his head, with the rimless cap thrust close on the shock of black hair, bent low; his hands thrust deep in the bulging pockets.

"A new live play-toy h'it may be,' ventured the father; "he is one funny chil."

The next day Titee was late for school. It was something unusual, for he was always the first on hand to fix some plan of mechanism to make the teacher miserable. She looked reprovingly at him this morning, when he came in during arithmetic class, his hair all wind-blown, his cheeks rosy from a hard fight with the sharp blasts. But he made up for his tardiness by his extreme goodness all day; just think, Titee did not even eat once before noon, a something unparalleled in the entire previous history of his school life.

When the lunch-hour came, and all the yard was a scene of feast and fun,

one of the boys found him standing by
a post, disconsolately watching a ham
sandwich as it rapidly disappeared down
the throat of a sturdy, square-headed
little fellow.

"Hello, Edgar," he said, "what you
got fer lunch?"

"Nothin'," was the mournful reply.

"Ah, why don't you stop eatin' in
school, fer a change? You don't ever
have nothin' to eat."

"I did n't eat to-day," said Titee,
blazing up.

"You did!"

"I tell you I did n't!" and Titee's
hard little fist planted a punctuation
mark on his comrade's eye.

A fight in the schoolyard! Poor
Titee was in disgrace again. Still, in
spite of his battered appearance, a severe
scolding from the principal, lines to
write, and a further punishment from
his mother, Titee scarcely remained for

his dinner, but was off down the railroad track with his pockets partly
stuffed with the remnants of the scanty
meal.

And the next day Titee was tardy
again, and lunchless too, and the next,
until the teacher, in despair, sent a nicely
printed note to his mother about him,
which might have done some good, had
not Titee taken great pains to tear it up
on the way home.

One day it rained, whole bucketsful
of water, that poured in torrents from a
miserable, angry sky. Too wet a day
for bits of boys to be trudging to school,
so Titee's mother thought; so she kept
him at home to watch the weather
through the window, fretting and fum-
ing like a regular storm in miniature. As
the day wore on, and the rain did not
abate, his mother kept a strong watch
upon him, for he tried many times to
slip away.

Dinner came and went, and the gray soddenness of the skies deepened into the blackness of coming night. Some-one called Titee to go to bed, and Titee was nowhere to be found.

Under the beds, in closets and cor-ners, in such impossible places as the soap-dish and water-pitcher even, they searched, but he had gone as completely as if he had been spirited away. It was of no use to call up the neighbors, he had never been near their houses, they affirmed, so there was nothing to do but to go to the railroad track where Titee had been seen so often trudging in the shrill north-wind.

With lanterns and sticks, and his little yellow dog, the rescuing party started down the track. The rain had ceased falling, but the wind·blew a gale, scurrying great gray clouds over a fierce sky. It was not exactly dark, though in this part of the city there is neither gas nor electricity, and on such a night as this neither moon nor stars dared show their faces in so gray a sky; but a sort of all-diffused luminosity was in the air, as though the sea of atmosphere was charged with an ethereal phosphorescence.

Search as they did, there were no signs of Titee. The soft earth between the railroad ties crumbled between their feet without showing any small tracks or footprints.

"Mais, we may as well return," said the big brother; "he is not here."

"Oh, mon Dieu," urged the mother, "he is, he is; I know it."

So on they went, slipping on the wet earth, stumbling over the loose rocks, until a sudden wild yelp from Tiger brought them to a standstill. He had rushed ahead of them, and his voice could be heard in the distance, howling piteously.

With a fresh impetus the little muddy party hurried forward. Tiger's yelps could be heard plainer and plainer, mingled now with a muffled, plaintive little wail.

After a while they found a pitiful little heap of sodden rags, lying at the foot of a mound of earth and stones thrown upon the side of the track. It was Titee with a broken leg, all wet and miserable and moaning.

They picked him up tenderly, and started to carry him home. But he cried and clung to the mother, and begged not to go.

"Ah, mon pauvre enfant, he has the fever!" wailed the mother.

"No, no, it's my old man. He's hungry," sobbed Titee, holding out a little package. It was the remnants of his dinner, all wet and rain-washed.

"What old man?" asked the big brother.

"My old man. Oh, please, please
don't go home till I see him. I'm
not hurting much, I can go."

So, yielding to his whim, they carried
him farther away, down the sides of the
track up to an embankment or levee by
the sides of the Marigny Canal. Then
the big brother, suddenly stopping, exclaimed :

"Why, here's a cave. Is it Robin-
son Crusoe?"

"It's my old man's cave," cried
Titee. "Oh, please go in; maybe he's
dead."

There cannot be much ceremony
in entering a cave. There is but
one thing to do, — walk in. This
they did, and holding up the lantern, beheld a weird sight. On a
bed of straw and paper in one corner
lay a withered, wizened, white-bearded
old man with wide eyes staring at
the unaccustomed light. In the other

corner was an equally dilapidated cow.

"It's my old man!" cried Titee, joyfully. "Oh, please, grandpa, I couldn't get here to-day, it rained all mornin' an' when I ran away, I fell down an' broke something, an', oh, grandpa, I'm all tired an' hurty, an' I'm so 'fraid you're hungry."

So the secret of Titee's jaunts down the railroad was out. In one of his trips around the swamp-land, he had discovered the old man exhausted from cold and hunger in the fields. Together they had found this cave, and Titee had gathered the straw and paper that made the bed. Then a tramp cow, old and turned adrift, too, had crept in and shared the damp dwelling. And thither Titee had trudged twice a day, carrying his luncheon in the morning and his dinner in the afternoon.

"There's a crown in heaven for that child," said the officer of charity to whom the case was referred.

But as for Titee, when the leg was well, he went his way as before.